BONE'S LAW

by

KEN FARMER

Cover by K.R. Farmer

FORWARD
by
Marshall R. Teague - Veteran Actor, Ret. Navy, former Deputy Sheriff

When I was a child. I dreamed of being a Cowboy in the old West. I read every book and watched every TV show that had my Western Hero's atop there mighty steeds, all of which had Great names like Champion, Trigger, Dollor, Topper, Tony, and Black Jack.

Today, having done Eighteen Western Films and Television shows, many of which were taken right out of the pages of Western writers of high acclaim. Writers like Louis L'Amour, Terry C. Johnston, Zane Gray and Ken Farmer, who have kept the Western lore very much alive now and for Generations to come.

Novelist, Ken Farmer, whose books I have become obsessed with, captures every element which draws the reader back in time and places them at the same camp fire alongside the many colorful characters that you feel you have always known. Names like Flynn, Fiona, Bass, Bone, Loraine and Lucy, just to name a few you will become very familiar with.

Don't be surprised if, along the way, you pick up a touch of Shakespeare, History...past and present, along with what one might say...A Look at Our Future...Saddle Up, You're in for *A Hell of a Ride*!

Marshall & Lindy Teague

ISBN-13: - 978-1-7329119-1-8
ISBN-10: - 1-7329119-1-6
Timber Creek Press
Imprint of Timber Creek Productions, LLC
312 N. Commerce St.
Gainesville, Texas 76240

Published by: Timber Creek Press
timbercreekpresss@yahoo.com
www.timbercreekpress.net
Twitter: @pagact
Facebook Book Page:
www.facebook.com/TimberCreekPress
Ken's email: pagact@yahoo.com
214-533-4964

AUTHOR

Ken Farmer didn't write his first full novel until he was sixty-nine years of age. He often wonders what the hell took him so long. At age seventy-seven…he's currently working on novel number twenty-four.

Ken spent thirty years raising cattle and quarter horses in Texas and forty-five years as a professional actor (after a stint in the Marine Corps). Those years gave him a background for storytelling…or as he has been known to say, "I've always been a bit of a bull---t artist, so writing novels kind of came naturally once it occurred to me I could put my stories down on paper."

Ken's writing style has been likened to a combination of Louis L'Amour and Terry C. Johnston with an occasional Hitchcockian twist…now that's a combination.

In addition to his love for writing fiction, he likes to teach acting, voice-over and writing workshops. His favorite expression is: "Just tell the damn story."

Writing has become Ken's second life: he has been a Marine, played collegiate football, been a Texas wildcatter, cattle and horse rancher, professional film and TV actor and now…a novelist. Who knew?

Ken Farmer's dialogue flows like a beautiful western river…it's the gold standard…Carole Beers

Web page: www.KenFarmer-Author.net

DEDICATION

This tome, is book #13 of The award-winning, The Nations Series and #3 of the spin-off Bone Series and is dedicated to one of my writing inspirations...**Edgar Rice Burroughs** -1875-1950. Best known for his iconic Tarzan and John Carter of Mars novels, but he also wrote four outstanding westerns...*The Bandit of Hell's Bend, The War Chief, Apache Devil and The Sheriff of Comanche County.*

Burroughs writes with great western authenticity partially from his experience as an enlisted soldier in the storied 7th Cavalry in Arizona in the 1890s plus an unmatched imagination.

There are a couple of quotes I especially like from ERB: "I have been successful probably because I have always realized that I knew nothing about writing and have merely tried to tell an interesting story entertainingly." Another is: "Am I alive and a reality...or am I but a dream?"

ACKNOWLEDGMENT

The author gratefully acknowledges Lt. Colonel Clyde DeLoach, USMC (Ret.) and novelist Mary Deal for their invaluable help in proofing and editing this novel.

TIMBER CREEK PRESS

CHAPTER ONE

MONTAGUE COUNTY, TEXAS

"What'n Sam Hill?" Thirty-five year old Sheriff Bruce Jamison saw a puff of white smoke across the Red toward the little river town of Leon in the Chickasaw Nation.

He reined his red roan gelding to the right of the wagon road they had been tracking along. A little over a half second later it felt like someone had dropped an anvil on his chest.

He looked down at a dime-size hole where the second button on the gray pinstriped shirt just above a black vest used to be. What was there now was a red stain slowly spreading outward from the hole.

The sound of a big bore rifle echoed across the Red River valley.

"Oh, damn," he said as he slipped left sideways from the saddle and fell to the dusty ground like a rag doll. The veteran lawman was dead when he landed at the edge of the rutted road.

The roan horse shied to the right when the sheriff's body hit the ground, spun around and headed back toward the barn and safety in Montague, the county seat of Montague County, Texas, at a gallop,

CLAY COUNTY, TEXAS

Sheriff Miles Bradford's black one-horse Phaeton buggy came to a stop in front of Cravens' Livery and Wagon Yard in Henrietta. The lathered black

Tennessee Walker pawed the ground impatiently to get inside to his stall and be fed.

The owner, Martin Cravens, stepped out of the wide alleyway of the large barn-like structure at the edge of town. He wore his usual clothes for the day, blue bib overalls over a faded red union suit and a crumpled brown fedora that had seen better days.

Cravens leaned the pitchfork he had been using to clean stalls against the side of the green board and batt building.

"Well, yer back early, Sheriff. Step yerself down an' I'll take care of Buck fer you an' put that buggy away. 'Peers he could use a good brushin', he's kindly sweated up...Sheriff? Sheriff Bradford, you awright?"

Cravens walked up to the driver's side of the well-kept carriage after tying the horse to a hitching post and looked more closely at the sixty something white-haired sheriff slumped in the seat. His dark gray Homburg was lying askew beside him.

The back of his head had cracked the isinglass window in the rear.

"Oh, Lordy, Lordy," Cravens exclaimed as he noticed the front of Sheriff Bradford's shirt and vest were soaked with blood.

He backed up a couple of steps, turned and headed for Doc Owens office in the next block.

SKEANS BOARDING HOUSE
GAINESVILLE, TEXAS

Detective Darrell Ulysses Bone reclined on the green settee in the parlor, scanning through the latest issue of the Gainesville Daily Register.

His partner, Inspector Loraine Rodriguez, was reading a novel in a burgundy wing back chair near the crackling fireplace. She was halfway through *The Picture of Dorian Gray*, by Oscar Wilde, loaned to her by the owner of the boarding house, Faye Skeans.

The two police officers had been slingshotted back in time 120 years through an ancient Native American portal in the Brazos River valley over a month earlier. They must wait until the occurrence of a blue moon next year in June before the ancient electromagnetic vortex portal is active again.*

STEELDUST - July 20, 2018

"Well, Pard, this is interesting," said Bone.

Loraine didn't look up. "What?"

"Says here that there have been two county sheriffs killed in the last week. Sheriff Miles Bradford of Clay County and Sheriff Bruce Jamison of Montague, County. Both shot from ambush...no leads." He looked down at the paper again. "No, hang on, here's something else...One of Jamison's deputies was also found bushwhacked at the edge of town...also by a high powered rifle."

Loraine finally looked up. "Oh, my, see what you mean. That is interesting...Think there's any connection?"

He glanced askance at her. "Now what do you think, Pard?...Both the high sheriffs of their county and one deputy...All three shot from ambush by a high powered rifle, no clues, no suspects...May have a serial killer here...a sniper. And I know snipers...Don't believe in coincidence, you?"

"You know I don't. May be a vendetta, too...So, what are you saying?"

"Saying we need to put our detective skills to use while we're still trapped here in this time line and check it out...before they work their way down to Jack County and Grandpa Flynn."

"Better not let him hear you call him that...or call your great grandmother, Fiona, Grannie...if you know what's good for you."

"Yeah, I know." He grinned. "Fiona'd peel my head like an onion...So, what do you think?"

"Think we should go check it out. I'm getting bored since we got back from the Kiamichis and helping Bass and them take care of that Teddy Roosevelt thing."

He grinned. "Thought you'd never bring it up." Bone got to his feet—all six foot eight of him. "What say we take a run over to Jacksboro and see what Mason has to say."

"Thought you'd never ask," said his very attractive, five foot three, ample breasted partner.

Bone arched his brows at her.

"I think we should change back into our buckskins if we're going out on the trail...Save these new duds we had made at that seamstress shop downtown for civilized work," commented Bone.

"Either that or our BDUs," replied Loraine.

"Hey, that's an idea, too, Pard. You do contribute somethings...on occasion."

"Damn you, Bone," she backhanded the big man across his broad chest. "You just have to say something, don't you?"

"Well, if you don't know what you don't know, how are you going to know what it is if you don't know until you know it."

"My God, more Bone logic." Loraine shook her head, swinging her shoulder length raven locks side to side.

He grinned that big grin of his and cocked his head slightly as he walked out the doorway to the foyer. "I know."

The copy of *The Picture of Dorian Gray* bounced off his back.

"Ow...Gonna lose your place, Pard," he commented without looking back from the bottom of the stairs as her bookmark landed beside the book on the floor.

CHICKS MERCANTILE
GAINESVILLE, TEXAS

Bone reined his dark chestnut seventeen hand half Friesian gelding in front of Chicks Mercantile.

Loraine did the same with her smaller sorrel Quarter Horse mare. They stepped down and tied off in the rings on the iron posts set in concrete.

"Another good idea, Pard, getting our trail supplies before we left town."

"I was afraid all you had in your saddlebags were tins of sardines, moldy cheese and stale crackers," Loraine replied and stepped up on the hand-cut limestone curb in front of the store.

"The staff of life."

"For you, maybe, but I prefer something more, lets say, nutritious…Like canned meat, a slab of bacon, beans, dried apples, pickled peaches and, of course, plenty of Arbuckles."

"Love me some pickled peaches…You gonna make a trail cobbler?" he asked.

"Dream on, Bone. It's only going to take a day and a half to get to Jacksboro."

"Just asking…Wonder if they got any Spam?"

"Didn't make Spam till just before WWII, Bone."

"Oh, dang…If it ain't Spam, it ain't ham." Bone raised both arms over his head like an orator up on a podium. "Man cannot live by bread alone…He gotta have Spam."

Loraine glanced over at the big man as he opened the right side of the nine foot front doors, ringing the two inch brass bell hung from the header. "God help me…What I have to put up with."

He bowed slightly. "After you, m'lady."

"You did that on the last crack house we busted in our time…I nearly got shot."

"Close only counts in horseshoes and hand grenades."

"Damn you, Bone," Loraine said as she headed down the canned foods isle.

"We best pick up a couple of sheepskin coats. It's starting to turn a bit chilly in the mornings."

"Much as I hate to admit it, you're right, Bone," she answered over her shoulder. "Glad we already thought to get Buck Stienke over at his Lone Star Shooting Supply to make us some more smokeless powder ammo for our weapons."

"Like we say in the Marine Corps…Can't never have too much ammo."

"That's something else I like about the Marines."

COOKE COUNTY

They waded their mounts across Cove Hollow Creek. The water was up to the horse's bellies. Bone and Loraine both had their feet up to keep their tall Apache style moccasins from getting wet.

"Nothing I hate more than wet feet," commented Bone.

"For once you said something I agree with," Loraine responded.

"Wonders never cease…I thought it was twice." Bone stuck his feet back in the two-inch wide leather-wrapped stirrups, raised up and looked around when they reached the other side. "You know, Pard, we just as well drop by Lucy and them's. We go right past there."

"I may fall out of my saddle."

He looked over at the raven-haired Hispanic beauty. "How so?"

"Another good idea…That's three in one day."

"Looks like you're behind, then, doesn't it, Pard."

"Just wait…Remember those hot coals in your blanket?"

"Well, I figure we'll be spending the night with a roof over our head...after some of Mary Lou's chicken and dumplins and peach cobbler. Along with some great company."

"Is that all you think about? Chicken and dumplings and cobbler?"

"They're staples...Especially when Mary Lou Wilson makes them."

"You have a point there," Loraine commented. "What do you think Mason will know about the shootings?"

"I'd be willing to bet he's already found out what those three law officers had in common."

"You don't think it's random?"

He glanced over at her as he nudged Hildebrandt, the name he had given his big gelding, into a smooth, slow, amble trot. "Not a chance, Pard, not a chance."

§§§

CHAPTER TWO

WILSON RANCH

Lucy, the tiny alien stranded when her spacecraft crashed at Aurora, Texas, April 17, 1897. She was masquerading as an abandoned child living with Sheriff Mason Flynn's sister and his brother-in-law.

Lucy jumped up from the stoop of the big wrap-around porch in front of the white dog-run style, 19th century, ship-lap home as Bone and Loraine rode into the property.

She ran to the picket fence that surrounded the front yard, opened the gate and jumped up into Bone's arms as he stepped down. Her yellow and white pit bull, Garin, followed her out the gate, wiggling all over and wagging his tail.

"Sensed ya'll were coming early this morning right after you crossed that creek...I've been sitting on the porch for over an hour." She glanced over at his partner. "Hi, Loraine...How's your new horse?"

"I like her, Lucy. She's really smooth...Named her Sweet Face."

"Why did you name yours Hildebrandt, Bone?"

"Well, being half Friesian, he looks like the horses the armored knights of old rode into battle. So, figured Hildebrandt was a good name from the fifteenth or sixteenth century...Besides, I saw it in a book I read, *The Crimson Amulet* by Adriana Girolami...about Templar knights and Muslims."

Loraine glanced at him. "You read?...Who knew?"

"Good one, Pard," he retorted.

Lucy grinned at the big man. "Only you, Bone, only you...Oh, Garin is glad to see ya'll, too."

Garin was dancing around both Bone's and Loraine's feet, waiting for attention.

"Well, come here big guy," said Bone as he knelt down and rubbed behind both ears of the muscular yellow and white pit bull.

Loraine joined him as Garin flopped over on his back for a belly rub.

"Got you trained, Pard," commented Bone.

"Yes, he does," Lucy commented.

"Bone...Loraine," came a woman's voice from the porch. "Ya'll come on in the house. Supper's almost ready. Lucy told us you were coming, so, I fixed your favorite."

"Chicken and dumplins?" responded a grinning Bone.

"Of course...along with a big peach cobbler."

Loraine grinned, too. "Now, who's got who trained?"

"Oh, yum," said Bone as he opened the spring-loaded gate for Lucy, Loraine, Garin and himself.

"...and that's the name of that tune," said Bone as he finished explaining to the Wilsons what they were doing this way. They had finished supper and Mary Lou filled the coffee cups again.

The comfortable ranch home, that would belong to Bone in 2014, still had the lingering odor of hot peach cobbler with a hint of cinnamon.

"Would you like for me to come along, Bone?" asked Lucy.

"No, hon, that's alright..." He smiled and glanced at Loraine. "...This is what we do. Right, Pard?"

"When you're right...you're right, Bone," she replied.

"And you're very good at it too. I told mother and father how you save the house from being burned down...and me killed in the future," commented Lucy.

"Hate people who break the law and try to hurt others...Won't stand for it. Good thing Captain St. John and I were out bird hunting and got onto Lucy's property...Might have never known about that disreputable greedy oil company harassing her until it was too late, otherwise." *

Legend of Aurora - May, 2014

"Just need to get to Mason. Don't know if he's on the shooter's list or not, but, I'm not going to take the chance...I have a lot of experience in hunting down snipers...I was one," stated Bone with a firm set to his jaw.

"You know my brother's not going to go into hiding, don't you?" asked Mason's sister, Mary Lou.

"I know, but, if we can keep him and Fiona distracted long enough...we'll find the shooter, trust me," said Bone.

"I hope so," said a troubled Mary Lou as she glanced at her husband, Cletus, and then stared out a window in the dining room.

"Mason's a hard man to kill, Bone," said Cletus Wilson.

"Know that too."

"Any way ya'll can get him and Fiona to come for a visit?" asked Loraine.

"Might have some ideas. Let me check them out," replied Cletus.

"Sooner, the better," said Bone. "We'll be in Jacksboro by noon tomorrow."

Cletus scratched his stubbled chin for a moment. "When I find out what I'm thinkin' about, I'll send a telegram from Roston."

BONE'S LAW

JACKSBORO, TEXAS
COUNTY SEAT - JACK COUNTY

Bone and Loraine trotted their horses into town from the northeast just a little after noon and pulled rein in front of Mom Tucker's Livery. The blue bibbed overall clad hostler strode from inside, smoking her corn cob pipe.

"Well, look who's here, Man Mountain and his keeper," said the stout fifty-five year old owner, with a grin. "What brings you to Jacksboro?"

"Just come for a visit to Mason and Fiona, Mom," replied Bone.

"You find 'em down to Ruth Ann's havin' lunch. If ya'll hurry, you kin join 'em...I'll take care of your mounts."

She turned to the open double-wide doorway and called to her teenage son, "Haircut!...Haircut, get yourself out here. Got customers." Mom turned back to Bone and Loraine as they dismounted.

"Thanks, Mom," said Loraine as she handed over her reins and they turned and walked down the street to Sewel's Restaurant.

The restaurant was three blocks from the Jack County courthouse at the center of town. It was a European style, four story native stone building with spires at each corner and a two story clock tower in the center. The iconic building was built in 1866.

Bone and Loraine stepped through the front door of the popular diner, ringing the brass bell overhead. They spied Mason and Fiona against the far wall at their regular table.

Deputy US Marshal Fiona Flynn was first to look toward the door to see them. The beautiful raven-haired woman shot to her feet and headed through the tables in their direction, with a big smile across her classic features.

"Bone, Loraine, what are ya'll doing here?" she asked as she hugged Loraine, and then Bone. "Come on over and sit...Have you had lunch yet?"

"Whoa, Fiona, one at a time. First, we came for a visit and second...No," replied Bone as they walked toward Flynn and their table.

Loraine leaned across to Fiona as they walked. "Looks like you're starting to show a little."

Fiona glanced at the much shorter woman and patted her slightly bulging stomach. "Oh, thank goodness...I thought I was getting fat."

Loraine nudged her on the elbow and grinned. "Oh, that's real funny Missus Flynn...Real funny."

"Bone...Loraine," Sheriff Flynn said as he rose to his feet. He shook Bone's hand, and then gave Loraine a brief hug. "Sit, sit." He pointed to two empty chairs at their table.

"So, what do we owe the pleasure?" asked Fiona.

Before Bone or Loraine could answer, Ruth Ann Sewell appeared at their table with her note pad. "Loraine, Bone...It's really nice to see you again. I'm assuming you haven't eaten yet."

"Thought you'd never ask, Ruth Ann. I could eat a bear," said Bone.

"You remember what happened the last time you said that," commented Mason.

"Ah, right...Teddy Roosevelt, the mountain lion, bear and big foot," retorted Bone.

"Excuse me?" questioned a puzzled Ruth Ann.

"Inside story," said Loraine. "What's the special today?...Not that it really matters. Everything you make is wonderful."

"I want to thank you again, Bone, for showing me how to make those pizza pies...I still run out of dough every evening...Now, the special today is battered pan steak and cream gravy, fried sweet potatoes, buttered squash, crowder peas and hot yeast rolls with apple pie for desert...That's fresh apples too...It's the season."

"Yum, sounds good to me," commented Bone. "You, Pard?"

"Oh, yes, replied Loraine. "My mouth is already watering...and I'll have sweet tea with a sprig of mint."

"Me too," added Bone.

"Mason, you and your lovely wife need a refill on your coffee?"

"I'm good," said Fiona.

"I could use a warmup, Ruth Ann...Just barely run it over," added Mason.

She looked at Sheriff Flynn, shook her head and headed to the kitchen.

"Now, to your question, Fiona." Bone glanced over at Mason Flynn, and then back at Fiona. "I'm assuming ya'll know about the three law officers murdered last week in north Texas."

"Four," said the sheriff.

"Four?" questioned Loraine.

Mason nodded. "Another deputy from Clay County...yesterday."

"Same parameters?" asked Bone.

"Identical," replied Fiona.

"Any other commonalties or connections?" inquired Bone.

Sheriff Flynn grimaced and nodded again. "We all rode in several posses together a few years ago...before I became a sheriff."

"We?" asked Loraine.

§§§

CHAPTER THREE

MONTAGUE COUNTY, TEXAS

Deputy Burton Emmons knelt down and studied the prints along the edge of the dusty road. He pursed his lips, nodded, stepped over in the grassy area of the shoulder, stabbed his foot in the stirrup, and swung his big frame into his Texas style, square skirted saddle.

BONE'S LAW

Burt reached into his vest pocket, pulled out his bag of Bull Durham makings and started rolling a cigarette. He licked the edge of the thin, tissue-like paper, twisted the ends and stuck the quirly in his mouth. Reaching in his other vest pocket, he extracted a strike-anywhere phosphorus match and popped his thumbnail over the top, exciting a hissing burst of a yellow flame.

As he raised it to his lips, he felt a hard burning thump to his barrel chest. He grunted, fell backward to the horse's croup, and flipped to the ground as the sound of a big bore rifle echoed across the grassland.

The unlit roll-your-own went flying one way, the still burning match the other. The match fell into the weeds at the side of the road and immediately the dry Fall grasses began to burn, sending a swirl of white smoke skyward.

The creeping fire inched toward Burt's boot and began curling about the tall riding heel. Its devouring flames licked around the leather setting it on fire after a moment, but Deputy Emmons couldn't feel it—he was dead when he hit the ground behind the horse.

Two miles away, in the small agrarian and cattle town of Bowie, the hostler of the livery on the southeast side noticed the smoke rising in the air to the east from where he was cleaning one of the corrals. "Uh, oh...Grass fire...Better git the boys."

SEWELL'S RESTAURANT
JACKSBORO, TEXAS

"There were seven of us...Called ourselves the Trackers..." Flynn grimaced. "Five have been killed...One last year and now..."

A redheaded teenager with a flat-topped Western Union and Cable cap entered Sewell's and came straight to the sheriff's table. "Telegram for you, Sheriff," he said. "Want me to wait?"

"Let me read it first, son."

Flynn ripped open the thin paper of the envelope, extracted the yellow flimsy and quickly perused the missive. He reached in his pocket, pulled out a quarter and flipped it to the young man.

"No answer, Willie,"

The messenger caught the quarter in the air. "Thank you, sir," Willie spun on his heel and headed back to the door.

Flynn looked at the others, flexed his jaw muscles, and then said, "Six."

"Dang. Where?" commented Bone under his breath.

"Same MO?" asked Loraine.

Mason frowned and nodded. "Montague County, bushwhacked outside of Bowie. East...Big bore. Grass caught fire when he dropped his cigarette or a match falling from his horse...Telegram said it wasn't pretty."

"Ya'll were kinda like Billy the Kid's Regulators, then?" asked Bone.

"Sorta...We would be deputized by whatever duly elected sheriff there was in the county in which the perpetrators committed their crime, usually some type of robbery, and went from there..."

"What was your territory?" inquired Loraine.

Flynn glanced at his wife, Deputy US Marshal Fiona Mae Miller-Flynn. "We would get deputized in Clay, Montague, Cooke, Wichita, Archer, Young, Jack, Wise, and Denton...Figured if we

25

didn't get 'em before they got out of that area or crossed the Red into OT or the Nations...We weren't goin' to."

"Who are the other five?" asked Bone.

"Well, let's see...Jim Brownlow, lived in Cooke County, Brady Johnson, Clay County, Clyde Merkins, from Wise County, Ronnie Meeks, also Wise County...and me...This is Clyde." He held up the flimsy. "And before you ask...Not goin' into hidin'."

Willie burst through the door again with another telegram and strode to the sheriff's table again. "'Nother telegram, Sheriff." He handed the yellow envelope over.

Mason did the same as before and read the message. "Hmm."

"Answer, sir?" Willie broke out his tattered pad and red stub of a number two pencil and licked the end.

"Who's it from?" asked Fiona.

"Cletus...Says he wants us to come over to look at the Manier place near them in Cooke County. Got a couple sections...The folks'er movin' to Fort Worth to live with the daughter...Gettin' out of the ranchin' business an' retirin'…lookin' to sell…Stock an' all."

"Didn't ya'll say you wanted to get some property in Cooke County, near your sister and them?" inquired Bone.

"You're the last one…Not letting you going to ride around this county making yourself a target, mister…I won't be a widow before our child is born."

"I know, honey, but I still have to do my job. Can't bury my head in the sand."

"Didn't you say you weren't going to run again?" asked Bone.

"I did," Mason answered.

"Well, you're holding the answer in your hands." Bone paused for a moment. "Tell you what, Mason. You deputize Loraine and me and we'll take over here…Got Gomer to help out. He's almost healed up from that beating old man Sinclair and his boys gave him."

"What about that killer that's on the loose?" Flynn asked.

"That's my point…You're on the list. We can start our investigation and find the guy…It's what we did up in our time, Sheriff…our speciality...Besides I was a sniper in the Marine Corps...I know how to hunt 'em, and he won't know who's after him...'Nuff said."

"Better deputize you as Deputy US Marshals, too. In case you have to go out of Jack County..."

Fiona glanced at the sheriff. "Doctor Visser wants me to take it easy, now that I'm in my second trimester, darling...It's the most dangerous time for losing a baby, he says." Fiona drilled him with her steel-gray eyes that took on an extra hard glint. "I'll not loose another."

"What do you mean, another, Fiona?" asked Loraine.

She turned to the attractive Hispanic woman sitting at her right. "I was pregnant when Frank Miller and I were married. He was my first husband..."

"He was murdered by that Cherokee renegade, Cal Mankiller," interrupted Loraine.

Fiona nodded. "I was four months along when it happened." She stared blankly out the front window of Sewell's for a moment before saying softly, "I lost the baby." Fiona turned back to her husband. "It's not going to happen again, Mason Flynn...I've had my final say." She stared again, unblinking, at him.

The sheriff turned to Willie, who was still patiently standing next to the table and getting somewhat embarrassed, with his notepad. "Send this: CLETUS WILSON...stop...TELL MARY LOU AND LUCY WILL BE YOUR PLACE TOMORROW NOON...stop...WILL LOOK AT MANIER PLACE stop MASON AND FIONA...End." He pulled out a Morgan silver dollar and handed it to the young man. "Keep the change, Willie."

"Yes...sir!" he replied with a big grin, turned and headed toward the door.

The sheriff turned almost sheepishly to his wife. "Reckon we'd best go rent a buggy from Mom...sweetheart."

She placed a hand on his arm as her eyes softened, words weren't necessary.

"Can you make us a list of the miscreants your posse hunted down and the outcome of each before you go?" asked Bone.

The sheriff nodded. "Do it this afternoon...an' swear ya'll in, before we go out to the ranch to pack."

"We can get the buggy, but I want to also take Spot and your new horse, Sailor...If I do need to ride, his smooth as silk natural single foot will be safe for me," said Fiona.

Loraine turned to Mason. "Why did you name your new horse, Sailor?"

He grinned. "No horse will ever take Laddie's place, but Sailor is comin' close. He's a 16 hand lineback grulla saddlebred with a perfect rockin' chair lope...Feels like you're on a boat."

"Beats Hildebrandt, I suppose," Loraine replied, glancing at Bone.

Bone feigned a shocked look. "I like Hildebrandt...Besides how would it look for a guy like me to be riding a horse named Sweet Face...like yours?...Be almost as bad as naming him Puddin'."

"Point." Loraine nodded and looked up as Ruth Ann set their plates in front of them.

"Bring the pie when you're done with this...Got ice cream today to go on top," she said.

"Oh, yum," Bone exclaimed as he leaned over and took a deep whiff of the steaming breaded pan steak, covered in sawmill gravy.

BONE'S LAW

"You'd say 'Yum' if it was cat's ass and cabbage, Bone," commented Loraine.

His enigmatic grin slowly appeared on his face as he winked at her with one of his gold flecked eyes. "Yeah, but only if it was steamed with onions and mushrooms…Don't knock it till you've tried it, Pard." His grin got a little bigger. "Almost as good as roast possum with sweet potatoes."

"Oh, Lord…Sometimes you drive me crazy, Bone," his partner responded.

"I know."

SHERIFF'S OFFICE

"Now, these two were what was left of a gang of four brothers, the Waverlys, that we arrested after a three hour gunfight." Flynn held out two dodgers. "The two surviving brothers were hung by district Judge Leander Algernon Miles, III out of Cooke County."

"Any more family left? You know, cousins, uncles and so on?" asked Loraine.

"Just the mother…Name's Corine Waverly. She lives alone here in Jack County, south of Wizard Wells…an' is about seventy," replied the sheriff.

"Here's a possible. Cherokee Cobb…Judge give him ten years in Huntsville. Got out 'bout four months ago on good behavior after eight years. His baby brother was killed durin' the arrest."

"A definite person of interest," commented Bone. "Where's home?"

Flynn shuffled some papers. "Clay County, outside of Henrietta. Wife…" He looked down at some notes. "…June Cobb, one girl child, Susan. Would be ten 'bout now…She held everthing together while he was in the pen…Took in washin' an' did housekeepin' an' such for folks."

"You keeping notes, Pard?" asked Bone.

She looked up from her notepad with a 'Yes, stupid', expression.

"Right," said Bone.

"And one more…A Virgil Johnson, killed durin' the arrest. Left a wife, Thelma, an' son…Boy would be nineteen now…Name of Jessie James Johnson. They live up outside of Ardmore in the Chickasaw Nation, now." Mason looked over at Bone. "Could be a real angry young man."

Bone and Loraine exchanged glances.

"Could be," commented the big man.

"Interesting name in this day and time," added Loraine. "Jessie James Johnson."

§§§

CHAPTER FOUR

JACKSBORO, TEXAS

"Think it would be a good idea to send Jack and Selden a telegram up to Ardmore with the info on the widow Thelma Johnson and her son, Jessie James...Let Marshals McGann and Lindsey check them out," said Loraine.

"Yeah, save us a lot of time...not to say anything about the trip. We can focus on the ones in this area, like that Cherokee Cobb, fellow," commented Bone.

He wrote the information on a note pad from Sheriff Flynn's desk and handed it to the young deputy.

Gomer Platt, had been with Sheriff Flynn for a little over two years. He'd been wounded twice by outlaws and almost beaten to death by some others.

"Glad to see you're feeling better, Gomer," said Bone.

"How are the ribs?" asked Loraine.

He grinned. "Only hurts when I laugh...but it's like Sheriff Flynn always says..."

Bone interrupted him. "Well, it's either don't laugh...or can't keep a good man down."

Platt grinned. "Yessir...either or."

"When are you and Emma Lou getting married?" asked Loraine.

He blushed and looked at his feet. "Aw, she wants to before Thanksgivin', but that's next month...I kinda want to wait till maybe sometime in February or so...Been savin' ever dime I kin make so I kin rent a nice house here in town. The sheriff and Miz Flynn, sharin' some of the reward moneys with me occasionally, really helps...Ain't puttin' my Emma Lou in no shack...Even quit gittin' lemon drops from the mercantile."

"That's very noble of you, Gomer...Have you talked to Emma Lou about that?" asked Loraine.

"Uh...well, no ma'am. Figured that it was the man's place to provide for his family."

Loraine and Bone both smiled.

"Just a word to the wise, slick. Better include her in all those kind of decisions unless you want to live in mortal hell...Know what I mean?" commented Bone. "Now scat and get that telegram sent." He handed him a fifty cent piece. "Don't have to wait on an answer."

"Yessir." Gomer grabbed his battered slouch hat and hit the door.

"Where in the world did that come from, Bone?...You could have knocked me over with a feather," said Loraine after Platt closed the door behind him. "I thought you invented male dominance."

"What you get for thinking, Pard...Hey, I got a momma and pappa, too, you know...Seen my momma put more than one knot on my daddy's head for not clearing something with her before he did it...'Course it's my momma that's the grand daughter of Mason and Fiona...Plus my Padrino has mentioned it to me a time or two when I would start to spark some young lady." He grinned and shrugged.

Loraine shook her head. "Wonders never cease."

She strolled over to the potbelly stove in the corner, leaned over Sheriff Flynn's black and white Border Collie, Newton, taking his afternoon nap and filled her white ceramic mug. "Want some?"

"Thought you'd never ask," replied Bone as he stood up, walked over and handed her his cup.

"What if the shooter isn't one of those on the list?" Loraine asked as she poured his coffee.

"Good question, Pard...You had to bring it up, didn't you?"

"Somebody had to."

"Well, we start from scratch, then...looking for clues at the shooting sites and doing some good old fashioned gum shoe work...But, my gut tells me it has to be somebody connected with that posse," Bone said as he sat back down behind the sheriff's desk.

"Mine too," Loraine added as she took a sip of the stout brew.

"Whew, when did I make this?"

"I think yesterday…I just set it on the stove to warm it back up."

"Damn you, Bone," Loraine commented as she set her cup back down.

"All done, Mister Bone," said Platt as he came back in the front door.

"It's just Bone, Gomer…just Bone."

"Or Damn you, Bone, on occasion," commented Loraine.

Bone glanced at her, and then got back to his feet and walked over to the big multi-county colored map on the wall. He circled his finger around Henrietta. "Doesn't Mason's mother live somewhere close to this town?"

Gomer walked over and stuck his finger on a spot next to a creek about five miles north of the county seat. "Right here, Mis…uh, Bone. Nice lady. Met her a time or two…Easy to see where the sheriff gets his up-an'-gitum, never quit attitude."

"Uh, huh…Boy what I wouldn't give for GPS right now," said Bone.

"What's GPS?" asked Deputy Platt.

Bone and Loraine exchanged glances.

"Go ahead, Pard," said Bone. "You tell him."

She arched her eyebrows at him. "Stands for Global Positioning System..."

Gomer interrupted Loraine. "What?...What does that mean? I don't understand."

"I was getting to that," she continued. "Up in our time, Gomer, we have a system of satellites around the world that we can ask for the location of almost anyplace on Earth and find out where it is...and exactly how to get there."

"Satellite? You mean like the moon?"

"Well, sort of. It's a whole bunch of little machines that are put way up in the sky circling around the world...even though some of them are stationary over one spot..."

Bone interrupted Loraine. "What she means, slick, is they're moving at the same speed as the rotation of the earth, so, they give the appearance of being stationary...See?"

"No...But how do you git 'em up there an' is there folks inside 'em?"

"By rockets," said Bone. "...and no. It uses cameras and stuff like that...They're controlled from the ground.

"Aw...Like the ones they shoot off on the 4th of July?" He looked first at Bone and then at Loraine for a moment. "Oh, I git it...Ya'll 're funnin' me, ain'tcha?"

"Kid you not...But these rockets are just a little bit bigger than the ones you mentioned for Independence Day."

"If I didn't know ya'll were from the future, I'd think you were goofy as peach orchard boars...Little machines all up in the sky put there by rockets...Huh...Sorry I asked."

Gomer stepped over and poured himself a cup of coffee. "Wait'll Emma Lou hears this," he muttered and giggled. "She ain't gonna believe a word of it...I'm tellin' you."

Bone and Loraine both grinned.

"First thang she's gonna ask is how come they ain't fallin' down."

"That's a whole other deal, Gomer," said Bone as he handed the young deputy his cup for a warmup.

"Yeah...I'll bet." He grinned as he filled Bone's cup.

BONE'S LAW

FLYING L RANCH

Lisanne Gifford, astride her magnificent wild stallion, Steeldust, galloped across the north Texas grassland.

The sire of her breeding herd was striding effortlessly, his speed could top out near fifty miles an hour, but he could maintain this moderately paced gait of twenty-five miles an hour for more than forty-five minutes before needing to slow to a trot to catch his wind.

Steeldust's long black mane, frosted on the ends, was flowing in the wind. The blue-gray metallic shade of his coat showed a chatoyant shimmer in the late afternoon fall sun.

Steeldust's lineage went back to the Andalusian horses brought to America's shores by the Spaniards during the 15th century.

Certain isolated herds of mustangs or wild horses had maintained almost pure blood lines like the Kiger Mustangs of southeast Oregon over the centuries.

Lisanne's only control of the stallion were her hands holding on to the looped lead of a *mecate* at the base of his mane. The *mecate* was attached under his chin to a simple hackamore.

She only rode him bareback. Lisanne leaned forward far enough so her own long flowing blond locks blended with his mane like salt and pepper, as if they were one.

The wild stallion had never had a bit in his mouth or a saddle on his back, but allowed the seventeen year old teenager ride him to her heart's content. It was mutual and unconditional love.

The first time she ever rode him was for almost fifty miles in a little less than two hours to fetch *Annuna*, the diminutive stranded alien from the spacecraft crash at Aurora, Texas. She was masquerading as the Wilson's young daughter, Lucy, and could save Bone's life when he took a bullet meant for Fiona.

The steeldust stallion was used to running flat out for long periods as he drove his herd of wild mares across the prairie away from the cowboys and others constantly trying to capture them. Freedom was their life and they allowed only Lisanne to approach them.

The exhilaration of the ride almost caused her to not notice a dark figure up on the side of a rocky ridge overlooking the road to Sheriff Flynn's Broken Diamond F Ranch from town. It was only the glint from glass or a gun barrel that broke her reverie.

She bumped his horsehair *mecate* and relaxed her seat to signal Steeldust to slow to a walk, and then a full stop.

Lisanne focused on the distant figure for a moment, and then the dark image looked up at the honking from a skein of geese overhead heading to the south Texas coast for the winter, and then turned her way. The person apparently saw Lisanne and Steeldust staring their direction, turned back and clambered over the top of the ridge, silhouetting themselves against the late afternoon setting sun, and then disappeared from view.

"Uh, oh...That's not good, boy. We best go tell Mason and Fiona."

She made a kissing sound, squeezed her calves against his ribs, cueing the big stallion into a lope, and headed cross country toward the ranch house on the Broken Diamond F. Her spiritual connection to Steeldust was such that virtually all she had to do was think it and the horse would respond.

BROKEN DIAMOND F RANCH

Lisanne cued Steeldust to stop in front of the house.

"Sheriff! Marshal!" she shouted before the stallion had slid to a complete stop, drawing a perfect *eleven* in the dirt with his back feet.

Lisanne waited a moment as the dust cloud Steeldust had generated drifted past and Fiona came out the green gingerbread screen door.

"Lisanne, what are you doing here? Get down, get down."

She was joined on the big wraparound porch by Sheriff Mason Flynn.

"Well, hey, girl. Come on in," he said.

"Let me go water Steeldust an' be right back." She slid from the stallion's sweaty back and walked with him toward the long wooden water trough next to the barn.

Steeldust immersed his muzzle in the cool water and sucked up his fill. He lifted his head, water still dripping from his lips, and followed Lisanne into the adjacent corral where she threw him a flake of hay. She took a handful of the sweet prairie grass and rubbed him down with it.

"Be back in a bit, boy." Lisanne turned, climbed over the rail fence and headed back to the house where Fiona was waiting on the stoop with a glass of cool lemonade.

"Oh, wow, thank you...I need this," she said as she took a long drink.

"Now, to what do we owe the pleasure, Lisanne?" asked Flynn.

She took another sip of the lemonade, sat down on the top of the steps, pushed a long strand of her damp hair from her face, and looked up at them. "Steeldust an' I were out for a run an' saw somethin' glint from that ridge on the south 'tween town an' ya'lls place? You know, bout two miles from here?"

"Of course," said Mason.

"We stopped so I could take a better look...Knowed somethin' wasn't right. Saw a figure up in the rocks overlookin' the road. They looked up at a flock of geese flyin' south an' reckon they seen me an' Steeldust when they went to look back at the road...Well, then they turned an' slipped over the top of the ridge." She took another drink. "'Peered to me they had a long gun in their hands. I musta seen the sun glarin' off either the barrel or maybe even a scope er maybe they was wearin' glasses. Didn't git much more of a look than that…Figured ya'll oughta know." She drained her glass.

Mason and Fiona looked at each other for a long moment.

"Think this is the part where one of ya'll say something," quipped Lisanne.

Fiona started, and then turned to her. "We're thinking somebody wants to do Mason harm, Lisanne…I can't tell you how much we appreciate your information. We'll be heading to town in the morning to rent a buggy from Mom and going for a visit to Mason's sister and them."

"We'll go up the backside of that ridge and check it out before we head to town. If they're there again in the mornin', we'll have 'em," said the sheriff.

Lisanne nodded and smiled. "God help 'em then."

§§§

CHAPTER FIVE

MCGANN CABIN
ARBUCKLE MOUNTAINS
CHICKASAW NATION

Marshal Selden Lindsey pulled rein in front of Marshal McGann's large log home next to Honey Creek only a hundred yards from Turner Falls.

"Hello, the house," he yelled from outside the white picket fence around the front yard.

The screen door at the front of the house swung open. An attractive middle-aged woman with flaming red hair stepped out on the wide front porch holding a white dish towel in one hand and three year old towheaded Baby Sarah on her hip, as only mothers know how to do.

Ten year old Aurali Red, their other adopted daughter, came out right behind her.

"And ye might know ye'd be showin' up at me doorstep right at dinner time, ye blackguard, Marshal Selden Trullery Lindsey."

From inside came a familiar voice. "If that's Selden Lindsey out there, tell the scoundrel I'm not havin' any."

"The hell you say...We got work to do, Jack McGann...After some of Angie's dinner, that is."

"That's what I figured...I'll add some water to me red beans and ham and put on another skillet of cornbread."

She slapped her shapely thigh with the dish towel. "And ye'll eat what I got and like it, Selden Lindsey...Now take ye horse to the barn and tend to the poor mistreated creature, and then wash up and clean ye boots before you come in me house," Angie said in her Irish brogue. "Don't ye be makin' me take granda's *shillelagh* to ye."

"She'll do it too," came the voice again.

"I know," said Marshal Lindsey.

"I'll help you, Marshal Lindsey," said Aurali Red, so named because she, too, had flaming red hair like her adopted mother.

"Thank you, Aurali Red," Selden answered.

He headed to the barn leading Dan, his big black standardbred stallion to the water trough. He loosened the girth and Aurali Red threw him a flake of alfalfa from Jack's own fields on the hanging meadow above Honey Creek canyon after the ride from Ardmore, IT.

Instead of cleaning his boots, the black mustachioed, broad shouldered, Marshal Lindsey had pulled them off and left them sitting on the porch by the door.

"It's hopin' Son or Bear don't take them off and bury them, Selden Lindsey. 'Specially if they smell anything like ye whiffy feet," said Angie from the kitchen.

"Where are the big fellows, by the by?" asked Selden.

He and Jack were sitting at the dining table waiting for Angie to bring the hot cornbread for the red beans and bowl of fresh butter.

"Oh, they're out huntin' somewhere. Be back before we're finished with dinner...They both love cornbread," said Jack. "The big scudders know Angie's fixin' some."

As if on cue, there came a scratching at the front door.

"Speak of the boys," said Jack as he got to his feet and strode to the door. He opened it, then the screen door and stepped back.

"Well, come in, Son, an' you too, Bear."

The 180 pound white wolf-dog padded in without so much as a howdy-do and parked himself next Angie's empty chair at the table.

Bear, a black full blood wolf, sat down on the other side. Both turned their eyes toward the kitchen.

"See they know who's bringin' the food to the table...Surprised they don't want a plate with a knife an' fork," said Selden.

"What makes you think they don't?" asked Jack. "They're family."

Baby Sarah toddled over to him and threw her arms around Son's thick neck and hugged him. "My puppy."

"Aye, an' they're a lot less trouble than some others I know." Angie looked at Selden and then her stocky husband, her green eyes flashing with humor from the strong noontime light streaming through the window panes.

Jack scraped the last of Angie's special peach and apple cobbler from the bowl and licked his spoon, and then asked, "Now, what is this job of work we're needin' to do?"

Selden handed him the telegram from Bone. Jack took it, pulled his wire-rimmed glasses from a vest pocket and hooked them over his ears. He opened the envelope and read the yellow flimsy.

"Hmm, interestin'...Well, kiss a fat baby." He looked at Lindsey over the top of the glasses sitting on his nose. "You're gonna love this, Angiedarlin'...Thelma Johnson's maiden name is Dalton."

"Ye'd be joshin' me, husband."

"Nope, Bill an' them's cousin…Moved up to the Wallace place near Elk. You 'member, where we had that shoot out with Bill Dalton an' his gang?"

"Oh, I do indeed. Hard to forget," replied Lindsey.

"The Wallaces was cousins on the other side," said Jack.

"You shore they ain't Chickasaw? Seems like they're all cousins or somethin', too," commented Lindsey.

"Hello the house!" came the shout from outside.

"Speakin' of Chickasaw…sounds like me uncle, *Anompoli Lawa*," said Angie as she hurried to the door and stepped out on the porch.

"Uncle! Come on in the house, have some beans an' ham an' cornbread left…Me husband an' Marshal Lindsey will see to ye horse and buggy."

She looked back over her shoulder at the two men, who grinned and nodded.

"Yes, dear," said Jack as he reached back grabbed his hat from the pegs beside the door and stepped out on the porch, followed by Selden.

"Hey, Uncle," said Jack.

"Doctor Ashalatubbi," Selden tipped his black hat to the venerable Chickasaw physician and tribal Shaman.

"Jack, Selden…Good to see ya'll. Didn't know you were coming up today, Marshal Lindsey…and how are my girls?" He bent over and hugged both of them.

"I didn't either, till I got a telegram from Bone," he replied.

"Uncle *Anompoli Lawa*, I've missed you," said Aurali Red.

"You can tell me about it when you get back from tending to Sally." He handed Jack the lead rope to the copper sorrel mare hooked to the front of his buggy.

"Easy enough," said Jack as he and Selden headed to the barn with the horse and buggy.

"And I've missed you, too, *Issi' Homma'*, Little Red Deer," said the Shaman.

Angie took her uncle's black open crown Stetson with the traditional Red Tail Hawk feather in a bead and quill hat band and hung it on the pegs just inside the door.

After Jack and Selden had tended to Doctor Ashalatubbi's mare and filled him in on the telegram from Bone, they were all enjoying a cup of Angie's strong coffee out on the porch.

"I've had to go up to Elk a time or two to doctor the Johnsons. Thelma had a bout of the croup and her son broke his arm getting thrown by his horse."

"When was that, Uncle?" asked Jack.

"Oh, the boy, Jessie James...guess it was a couple of years ago and his mama, just last year...I can tell you this, they're both a little taciturn."

"Taciturn? Is that a Chickasaw word, Doctor Ashalatubbi?" asked Selden.

The white-haired Shaman chuckled. "No, it's English, Marshal...Means tight-lipped, don't say much...and I suppose you could say they're both a bit irritable, too...Don't associate with their neighbors much."

"That would go along with being taciturn, it would," added Angie as she rocked with Baby Sarah on her lap.

Aurali Red sat on the steps playing with her rag doll.

"I suppose so," said *Anompoli Lawa*, which was his Chickasaw name, meaning 'He Who Talks to Many'."

Jack and Selden exchanged glances.

"Would you say the boy could be called angry at the world for his daddy gittin' himself killed, Doctor Ashalatubbi?" asked Marshal Lindsey.

"Well, one, I wouldn't call him a boy anymore…He's nineteen. But, I think one could say he's definitely an angry young man." He took a sip of his coffee.

"Guess we need to take a ride over to Elk, then, Sel."

"Thought you'd never bring it up…First thing in the mornin'?"

"I'd say," answered Jack.

SHERIFF'S OFFICE
JACKSBORO, TEXAS

"So, that's what I saw yesterday evenin'. Didn't go up there, but I can show you 'bout where they was…Wadn't nobody there when I rode past comin' to town this mornin' from the Broken

55

Diamond F," said Lisanne. "The sheriff an' Fiona are down to Mom's gittin' a buggy."

"Yeah, they said they were going to do that. Want me and Bone to keep an eye on the Broken Diamond F," said Loraine.

Bone glanced over at her. "Well, Pard, sounds like we got a reasonably fresh, almost crime scene...I suspect we should go check it out."

"Think so too. I'll get that little crime scene investigation kit we made up," said Loraine.

"I'll head on down to Mom's and get our steeds saddled...Don't take all day."

"I'll be there right on your heels...It's in the desk drawer where you watched me put it." She opened the drawer and set the small box on the desk.

Willie from Western Union and Cable came in the front door just as Bone was getting to his feet.

"Telegram, Mister Bone." He jerked his flat topped hat from his head when he saw Loraine. "Ma'am."

"And it's just Bone, son."

"I'm going to be like Fiona, Willie...Don't call me, ma'am. You can call me Loraine or Inspector Rodriguez."

"Uh, yes...ma'a...uh, Inspector." The redheaded, freckled-faced young man turned a bright shade of pink as he handed the telegram to Bone.

Willie whipped out his note pad and stub of a pencil and stood waiting on Bone to read the missive.

"Well, this is interesting, Pard." He continued perusing the telegram.

"Are you going to tell me or am I going to have to stand here all day?"

He grinned. "Oh, right...This is from Winchester Ashalatubbi. Says Jack and Selden headed over to Elk to see the widow Johnson and her son...Seems her maiden name is Dalton." He looked over at her. "As in the Dalton gang?...Cousins."

"Really?"

"She's living in the house where Selden and Bass had the shoot out with Bill Dalton...Where Selden killed him...Shot him in the heart."

"Oh, my! How did you know that?"

"Uh...I got a book about him, *Selden Lindsey, US Deputy Marshal...The Man Who Killed Bill Dalton* written by his grandson, Harrell McCullough."

"I'm still amazed that you read so much, especially books without pictures…but that is interesting…We still need to check out the Cobbs and that Waverly widow," said Loraine. "You think it's possible that the Johnson boy could have come all the way down here from Elk?"

"It's known as Poolville in our time and it's on the south edge of the Arbuckles and sure…I suspect it's only about a two day ride from there to here."

"If we're lucky, we can pick up that potential shooter's tracks once we get out to the ridge," said Loraine.

"Too bad Bass isn't here, I think he could track a fish up the river…But, he taught me a few things I think we can put to use."

"Such as?" asked Loraine.

"Such as he can tell the difference between whites, blacks, Indians, Mexicans and Chinese just by their scent."

"Get out of town."

"True…Said the Seminoles he lived with could tell the difference between individuals in the tribe."

"Imagine he could find you blindfolded in a crowd."

"Not talking about body odor, Pard. Talking about scent…In your case it would be easy."

"Oh, how so?"

"One, you're a woman and two, you're a Mexican."

"Well, for your information, jarhead, I use rock alum crystal. Found out that's what folks use in this time as an excellent deodorant…instead of perfume, like the French did in the fifteen and sixteen hundreds."

"Maybe you should take it out of the wrapper next time," he quipped.

"Damn you, Bone."

§§§

CHAPTER SIX

MOM'S LIVERY
JACKSBORO

"This is a telegram we got this morning from Doctor Ashalatubbi." Bone handed the flimsy to Sheriff Flynn.

He and his wife, Fiona, were at Mom's getting the buggy to drive out to his sister's ranch in Cooke County. The buggy was in front of the livery barn.

Mom's son, Haircut, was tethering Fiona's paint John mule, Spot, and Mason's line back grulla gelding, Sailor, to the back of the buggy.

Fiona stepped over next to Loraine as Mason was reading the missive. "What is it?"

"Telegram from Winchester. Jack and Selden went out to talk to the Johnson widow..." He handed the telegram to his wife.

"Oh, my, my. Every day brings a new adventure...Related to the Daltons." She looked up at Mason, then Bone and Loraine. "Gets more interesting all the time."

"I'd say," said the sheriff.

"Loraine and I are heading out to that ridge and inspect the scene where Lisanne saw that person with the rifle...Made up what we call a CSI kit."

"CSI?" asked Fiona.

Loraine smiled. "Crime Scene Investigation...It contains, among other things, a powerful magnifying glass, a mirror, powdered graphite, small paint brushes to dust for possible finger prints. We got some surgical tape from Doctor Mosier..."

"What do you use the mirror for?" asked Fiona.

"To reflect light. If we want to see something in a better detail, we just bounce extra light to it," answered Bone.

Mason looked at Loraine. "What about the tape?"

"When we dust for fingerprints...the oils in a person's skin will stay for quite a while on things they touch...the graphite will show it...We lay a short strip of the tape over it, the powder sticks and we have a record of the perpetrator's prints which we can match up to a suspect and that..."

Fiona interrupted this time. "Tells you if they had been at the scene or not."

"Correct," said Loraine. "Of course, sometimes the surface isn't conducive to collecting prints...like on a rough rock or wood surface. However, if it's smooth...we get a print."

"Amazing," commented the sheriff.

Loraine held up a green bottle. "This is a dilute solution of phenolphthalein we got from the Jack County Apothecary..."

"A dilute solution of what?" queried a confused sheriff.

"Phenolphthalein is the proper name. The local apothecary or pharmacist uses it as part of a formula for bitters…"

"Oh, for constipation or dyspepsia," Mason interrupted Loraine again.

She nodded. "We use a diluted solution of it to detect traces of blood. If we sprinkle some on boards or clothing, even if its been washed…It'll show up pink. Very handy in CSI."

"Ya'll are givin' me a headache," said Flynn.

"Police work becomes very scientific, I see. It had a big boost with Eugène François Vidocq in the early 1800s. He is considered by many to be the father of criminology," stated Fiona. "He said, 'No matter how careful someone is, they will leave something at the crime scene…a hair, fiber, fingerprint, something…'You just have to know how to look for it."

"Oh, you know of Vidocq?" asked Loraine.

"Oh, yes, he inspired Sir Arthur Conan Doyle to create Sherlock Holmes," replied Fiona. "Along with Doctor Joseph Bell, a renown forensic scientist at Edinburgh University in England."

Bone looked at the sheriff. "What say we just go catch the bad guys, Sheriff?"

"Damn, was hopin' you'd say that."

"All that has its place, but nothing beats catching some outlaw in the act or with the goods...and that's what I intend on doing. We'll back it up with the fingerprints and blood work, if needed," said Bone.

"Lisanne's going to show us where she saw the figure with the rifle and we'll scout around for signs...She's waiting for us down at your office."

"And with what you taught me about tracking, Mason, we'll see which way the tracks lead...Be a good indication if they lead north toward the Red River and the Nations," said Loraine.

"Well, north includes the Cobb family in Clay County."

Loraine nodded. "True...but it would tell us which direction to go next."

"Look for cigarette butts, too. There's a difference between Prince Albert and Bull Durham," offered Fiona. "Bull Durham is darker...stronger."

"Good to know," answered Bone.

"And snuff spit is a lot thinner than chaw," added Mason.

"Something else we didn't know." Loraine glanced at Bone. "They don't chew or dip as much in our time, roll your own...or smoke period, for that matter."

"Mostly only cowboys and baseball players dip or chew now...I mean then...Actually I mean in the future," stammered Bone.

"We knew what you meant," said Fiona with a smile.

"Plus we can take a picture of the horse's tracks." Loraine held up her Galaxy 8 Smartphone.

"What's that?" asked Mason.

"We call it a *Smartphone*...Bone and I each have one. You know it's the future version of that machine Bell invented in your office...that you don't use...but these are portable...We can't use the telephone part in this time, but unit also includes a camera...See?"

Loraine took a picture of Fiona, and then turned it around and showed the image on the screen to Mason and Fiona.

"Oh, my, my. That's amazing," said Fiona.

"It also has a recorder we can use, but that's about it that functions in this time," said Bone.

"How do you give it power?" asked Mason.

"Well, normally it comes with a cord we can plug into a electrical outlet, but we didn't bring the cord or convertor, besides I'm positive it wouldn't fit the receptacles ya'll have here…But, in our time, Lucy added a small solar adapter to each of our phones…"

Fiona interrupted Loraine. "The sun supplies the energy and keeps your…*Smartphones*, I think you called them, working…at least the camera and recorder parts, like the bracelets you and Lucy wear…She explained the concept to us when we found her last year after her spacecraft crashed."

"Correct," said Bone. "We will be able to take a picture of any tracks we find and match the picture to any suspects…"

"Like the fingerprints," said Fiona.

"Correct again…Gran…" Bone stopped and then looked at Fiona and Mason and grinned. "You have no idea how hard it is to not call you grandmother and grandfather, now that you know who I am."

She and Mason looked at each other.

Fiona spoke up, "We understand. It's just that other people overhearing you might not…"

"And open a can of worms," said Bone.

"Precisely," agreed Fiona.

"Well, we're goin' have to hit the trail if we want to get to my sister's in time for noon dinner," said Mason.

"Ya'll keep your eyes open," said Bone as he hugged Fiona and shook Mason's hand.

"You too," replied the sheriff.

He helped Fiona up in the carriage.

"I'm not helpless yet, Mister Flynn," she retorted.

"I know, just being a gentleman."

"Oh, turning over a new leaf, are we?" Her steel-gray eyes twinkled.

He shook his head as he walked around to the other side, clambered in and sat down. "Can't win for loosin'." He snapped the reins over the sorrel's rump and clucked twice. "Come up there, girl."

Bone and Loraine watched them roll down the main street of Jacksboro, headed east.

"Well, shall we go, Miss Rodriguez?" asked Bone.

"Let's do it, Mister Bone," she replied.

They mounted and trotted down to the sheriff's office where Lisanne and her red roan filly, Strawberry, waited.

She had let Steeldust go back to his herd of mares and brought one of the fillies she had been training from her ranch, the Flying L.

Lisanne sat on the green slat-back bench by the front door with Newton at her feet as she waited on

Bone and Loraine. She jumped up as they dismounted.

Lisanne opened the door to the office. "You stay here with Gomer, Newt. You don't need to go with us. Go lay down where it's warm next to the stove.

She buttoned her coat as a dry cold front had rolled in this morning. It wasn't over forty degrees.

Bone and Loraine both had their sheepskin jackets on over their buckskins.

"Told you it was going to get a bit nipply didn't I, Pard…."

"I hate to agree with you about anything, Bone…It gives you a bigger head than you usually have, but, in this case…you're right. This wind can cut right through a person."

"How did you find a jacket that could button over your hooters?"

"Damn you, Bone." She looked around for something to throw at him, but since she was sitting on Sweet Face, there was nothing. "You just wait."

He shrugged and got that enigmatic grin of his. "What they all say."

BONE'S LAW

RIDGE OUTSIDE OF JACKSBORO

"It's right up there by that big rock about the size of an outhouse." Lisanne pointed.

Bone and Loraine dismounted and handed their reins to her.

"Don't see anything close to tie them to," said Bone.

"If you'll bring them out to the ranch, I'll teach them to ground tie," Lisanne commented.

"My horses back home would do that, took me a couple of months to teach them," he said.

"I can do it in about two to three weeks. It's pretty easy and really is better for them if they have to move for their own safety."

"Sounds good to me," added Loraine as she got the CSI kit from her saddlebags.

She and Bone worked their way up the rocky ridge toward the big boulder, watching for tracks as they went.

"Hey, hey, looky here, Pard...footprints. Take a picture."

Loraine took out her phone, focused for a close-up of a left foot print, and then of the right. "Hmm, not too large, Bone. About a size nine, max...but it has a small flat heel."

"Boy? Small man?"

"That'd be my guess," she replied.

They reached the area behind the boulder looking over the road below.

"Ah, ha!" Bone exclaimed. "Something else already."

"What?" asked Loraine.

"Snuff spit...too thin to be chewing tobacco, according to Flynn. Take a picture."

"Aye, aye, Captain, sir. At your direction, sir...Consider it done, sir..."

"All right, all right, don't wear it out."

"Over here, Bone...Looks like they had to take a leak." She pointed at an area in the sand that was still damp with a quarter-size hole almost in the center.

He stepped over and looked at the spot. "Huh, must have really had to go. Hell of a splatter radius...unusual he didn't pee on the side of that rock there."

"Uh, huh...Was up here for a while, too. Area pretty well tracked all over," commented Loraine.

§§§

CHAPTER SEVEN

SHERIFF'S OFFICE
JACKSBORO, TEXAS

"Where did the tracks lead, M...uh, Bone?" asked
Gomer as he warmed up his coffee at the potbellied
stove in the corner. Newton looked up at him as he
filled his cup.

"Back down to the road. Lost them in all the other traffic," he answered. "Bass Reeves might could have followed them, but we couldn't."

"We'll know them the next time or maybe when we go interview the Cobbs and the widow Waverly," said Loraine.

"Goin' to see the Cobbs first?"

"Guess so, their place in Clay County is closer, isn't it?" asked Bone.

Deputy Platt walked over to the big map and pointed to an area. "'Cordin' to Sheriff Flynn, should be right here...near'bouts, east of Bluegrove...'Round thirty-five miles."

The front door to the combination sheriff's office and jail opened and Willard Barton, the swamper at the Coolwater Saloon ran in. He looked around first at Bone behind the sheriff's desk, then at Loraine sitting on the corner and finally he settled on Gomer still standing at the map.

"What is it, Willard?"

Deputy Platt, you gotta come quick, four of the Box R bunch 're in the saloon rasin' hob...Somebody's fixin' to git hurt."

"We got it Gomer," said Bone as he rose from the swivel chair.

"Who's he?" Willard pointed at Bone.

"Uh, that's Deputy Bone an' his partner, Deputy Rodriguez...Uh...Sheriff just hired 'em on 'fore he an' the missus had to go out of town."

"Well, never the matter...We gotta git back down to the Coolwater 'fore the shootin' starts."

"Want this scatter gun, Bone?" asked Platt.

He grinned and shook his head. "Don't see that it's necessary, Deputy. We'll be back in a short, short...Ready, Pard?"

"Waiting on me, you're backing up, Bone, you know that," said Loraine as she stood up.

"I know...Willard, is it?" asked Bone.

"Uh, yessir, Willard Barton...sir," he replied as he looked up at the big man.

"Why don't you stay here and keep Deputy Platt company...This won't take long."

Bone opened the door, grabbed his John Bull hat from the peg, shoved it on his head and gave it a jaunty cock to the right. "After you, Pard."

Loraine nodded as she stepped out on the porch. "Show time."

They sauntered down the plank boardwalk the two blocks to the Coolwater Saloon.

"Wonder if the saloon drinkers are any brighter in this day and time than the honky-tonkers are in ours?" queried Loraine.

"Probably not…Suspect most of them have a terminal case of the stupids, too," replied Bone.

"Hereditary?"

"Uh-huh."

"Who'd you say that big son of a gun was, now, Gomer?" asked Willard.

"Uh, he an' his partner there, Loraine Rodriguez are, uh…from out of town an'…"

"Well, hell, Gomer, figured that they wuz from outta town all by myself…My question is *who* are they?"

"Uh, alls I know is they're friends of the sheriff an' Fiona…end of story." Gomer nodded his head one time, firmly.

Willard looked askance at him. "You say so." He looked back to the closed door.

COOLWATER SALOON

Loraine opened one of the nine-foot doors, with the top half glass panels, that were closed during the colder fall and winter days. Then she pushed the batwing doors open and stepped inside the dimly lit smoky saloon. She moved to the left, Bone followed, closed the outer doors behind him, and slid right out of the backlight from outside shining through the glass. They waited for a moment for their eyes to adjust to the light.

"Saloons and honky-tonks all smell the same, don't they?…No matter what time period it is," said Loraine.

"Yep, stale beer, cigarette smoke, vomit and urine…My kind of place."

They walked down the bar to where four cowboys were standing and talking the loudest.

"Hey, barkeep, thought I told you to bring a bottle an' leave it," said the biggest one.

Truman Murphy, the slim, middle-aged, balding bartender and owner of the Coolwater Saloon stepped in front of the loudmouth customer on the other side of the thirty-five foot bar.

"Uh, don't you think you boys have had enough, Bull?"

The six foot two, heavyset cowboy reached across the polished surface of the bar, grabbed the bartender by the red cravat tied around his neck with his left hand and pulled him almost halfway across. "Now you listen to me, wet goods pusher, when we order a drink, I expect you to be Johnny on the spot...Got me?"

Bull pulled his Colt and stuck the muzzle under Truman's chin.

"Got me?" he repeated.

"Yes, sir...I got it. If you'll let go, I'll get your bottle for you."

"The good stuff, too. Not that back room bluestone, bug juice you usually try to give us.

"Yes, sir. Right away, sir," said Truman.

Bone took a step toward Bull, who still had his .45 in his hand.

Loraine stuck out her arm across his chest. "This one's mine, Bone...You got the last one."

"As you wish, Madam." He stepped back with a grin and allowed her to move up beside Bull and his friends.

"I think Truman said you boys have had enough...Bull. How about a cup of coffee instead...or a big glass of buttermilk...my treat," said Loraine as she leaned her right elbow on top of the bar.

Bull wheeled around and dropped his gaze down so his six foot two height even emphasized more Loraine's five foot three.

"Who the hell 're you?" he slurred. His gaze dropped even more to her bust.

She and Bone had changed from their buckskins to their camo BDU trousers and olive drab Ts.

"Deputy Sheriff Rodriguez...Now, how about that coffee or buttermilk?"

"Haw! A Mescan deputy sheriff an' a runt split-tail at that. Haw again...Why don't you go play with yer dolls, little girl?" He poked the muzzle of his pistol into her chest between her ample breasts several times, emphasizing his point.

"Ooo...mistake," said Bone sotto voce from behind her.

Loraine looked back at him and shrugged. "I tried."

She moved her right hand over the top of Bull's pistol and smoothly wrenched it from his hand and flipped the Colt over her shoulder where Bone caught it in the air.

"Hey!" said the surprised cowboy.

He made his second mistake and tried to grab her shoulder with his left hand. Loraine easily stepped to the side, grabbed his wrist with her left hand. She applied pressure against the side of the joint with her thumb, stepped back slightly and used his own weight and lack of balance to jerk him to the floor on his knees.

She stepped back, smiled and crossed her arms over her bosom. "Had enough?"

"Damn you." Bull lunged to his feet and swung a haymaker right at the side of Loraine's head.

She slipped the punch, grabbed his elbow on the way by and assisted his momentum to carry his two hundred and twenty pounds crashing into an empty round poker table with four chairs. Two of the chairs flipped backward as the table tipped over and landed on top of the confused cowboy.

Jumping up again, he grabbed one of the chairs, raised it over his head to bring it down on top of Loraine.

Once more, she smoothly ducked under his extended arms, slipped behind him bringing her own right over and on top of his like a professional defensive end football player's swim move, causing him to slam the chair into his left knee.

"Ow, ow, ow," he cried as he dropped the chair and fell to the floor holding his leg.

"You sure you want some more?" Loraine said.

Bull just growled, got to his feet and charged bull-like at her, mimicking his namesake.

And like a matador, the petite woman effortlessly spun out of his way, grabbed the back of his shirt collar as he passed and redirected him to slam headfirst into the side of the oak paneled bar.

Bull crumpled down onto the foot rail at the bottom like a pile of wet laundry and turned a full brass spittoon over onto his back.

The other three Box R cowboys looked down at an out cold Bull lying in a puddle of tobacco spit and phlegm, and then looked up at Loraine still smiling, standing with her arms crossed over her bosom once more. They looked down at Bull again, back at Loraine and finally back down to their friend.

"Bull?" said one of the cowboys tentatively. "Bull...you awright?"

"He's out like a light, Slim...Cain't hear you," said one of the others.

Loraine glanced over at the three friends and took a step toward them.

The rapidly sobering cowboys backed up in unison, all three holding their palms out in front of them.

"We're powerful sorry...Ma'am. He didn't really mean no harm," said Slim.

"One, don't call me, Ma'am. You can call me Deputy Rodriguez and two, get him on his feet and clean up that mess...Understand me?...You don't want me to say it twice. It wouldn't be pretty."

She turned to the bartender. "Truman, get these boys some towels, a mop and four glasses of buttermilk...on me."

Truman grinned like a Cheshire cat. "Be a pleasure, Deputy Rodriguez...an' the buttermilk's on the house." He bent over and pulled a stack of almost white towels out from under the bar and laid them on top. "Be right back with a mop fellers."

"You bet. We'll be right here," said Slim as he leaned over and assisted a groggy Bull to his feet.

"What happened?...Did I win?" he asked Slim.

"Not hardly...You G'd when you shoulda Hawed, Bull, an' run into a lady buzz saw."

"Huh?" He glanced at Slim, and then at Loraine, then back at Slim. "Oh...yeah...Is she gonna hurt me again?"

"Don't think so, Bull. Long as we clean up this mess and switch to buttermilk."

Bull looked up. "Oh, thankee, Lord. I'll never drink no forty-rod poteen no more...Promise on my sweet mama's grave." He turned to Slim. "Where's that buttermilk?"

Bone glanced over at a still grinning Loraine. "Nice work, Pard."

"So that was some of that Kung Fu stuff, you were talking about," said Bone as they headed down the boardwalk back to the sheriff's office.

"Yep...Beats a killing every time...Too much paperwork...Who knows, maybe they learned a lesson."

"Till they sober up...You know, Pard, how about you give me a few of those Kung Fu lessons?...You said you were a black belt?"

"Uh-huh, seventh degree...And I would dearly love to give you a few lessons, Bone...An-y-time."

Her face broke into a huge enigmatic smile of her own as they walked. An image and the sound track of Dick Dastardly's canine sidekick, Muttley, the laughing dog cartoon with his mischievous, wheezing laugh, blossomed in her mind.

§§§

CHAPTER EIGHT

WILSON RANCH
COOKE COUNTY

"The Manier property looks great," said Mason.

"Loved the house, too," added Fiona. "And that clear, rock-bottomed, year round creek that runs through the property is beautiful."

"Not counting the fact that it adjoins our property on the east," commented Mary Lou. "Make it handy when you need a baby sitter." She smiled.

Mason and Fiona exchanged looks and grins.

"Do you want to make an offer, Hon?" he asked.

"I think two dollars and fifty cents an acre is a fair price...inluding the stock," Fiona replied.

"Just hope Bone and Loraine catch whoever's killing the members of your posse," said Mary Lou.

"Especially before they get around to shootin' at Mason," added Cletus.

"Don't think there's anything to worry about on that matter," stated Lucy.

"Why do you say that?" asked Mary Lou.

"The wonderful Chickasaw Shaman, *Anompoli Lawa*, explained it quite well recently...He said that as a matter of ancient American Indian philosophy...'If you travel to the past through one of their portals, then you are part of the past...and always have been'. I think the mere fact that Bone and Loraine are here...and that they will be successful in apprehending the person or persons who are systematically murdering the members of that posse, says it all."

"I don't understand, Lucy," said Cletus.

Mason shook his head. "Me neither."

"Count me in that, too," agreed Mary Lou.

"If they are here, it means they've always been here and are part of our lives. It was foreordained that Bone would take that bullet meant for me and that Lucy and I would save him...or he wouldn't be here. Don't you see?" stated Fiona.

"No," said Cletus, Mason and Mary Lou simultaneously.

"It's simple to say...He just wouldn't exist...ever," added Fiona.

"Also, Bone would already know, since he's from the future, that his great grand father wasn't murdered...It's a matter of his history and time line," said Lucy. "And that he and Loraine are probably the reason why."

"What if somethin' happens to Bone?" asked Mason.

"If it does...like it did when he was shot...He will survive...and that's where I come in. I'm a part of Bone's life...and always have been."

"Lucy, I think I need you to work on this headache I just got," said Mason.

Cletus nodded. "Me too."

"Uh-huh," added Mary Lou, as she rubbed her temples.

Lucy smiled. "Not to worry, it's a concept that's still being discussed on my world of Tyrin...There are multiple paradoxes involved in time travel and they may never be solved."

"I think we just may have to accept the fact that it is what it is...always has been and always will be," said Fiona. "A 13th century work by the Persian writer Rumi was titled, *Fihi Ma Fihi*."

"Which means?" asked Mason.

"*It Is What It Is*," said Fiona, winking. "So not to worry."

Fiona and Lucy both smiled and looked at one another.

ARBUCKLE MOUNTAINS
ELK, CHICKASAW NATION

Marshals McGann and Lindsey pulled rein in front of the small four room log cabin that had belonged to the Wallace brothers. It was formerly the hideout of Bill Dalton.

They both were wearing their trail jackets with black woolen scarves about their necks against the fall chill. Selden's coat was a tan and Jack's a dark green canvas.

"Well, hadn't changed much," said Selden.

"Didn't realize we put so many bullet holes in the place durin' the shootout with Dalton and the Wallaces," commented Jack.

"Bullets didn't go through them logs though, but played hob with the windows an' frames," added Lindsey.

"Halloo, the house," yelled Jack.

In a few moments, the plank door opened and a thin wisp of a woman in her mid-forties, but looked older, stepped out on the porch. She was wearing a worn gray cotton day dress and a stained white apron.

"Hep, ye?" said the once attractive woman, now showing the wear of many years of hard scrabble farming and irregular meals. Her dull mouse brown hair, streaked with gray was up in a tattered bun behind her head.

"Yes, ma'am, I'm Deputy US Marshal Jack McGann an' this is Deputy US Marshal Selden Lindsey...Mind if we git down?"

"Just as well. Yer here…Ain't got no coffee ner nothin' else to offer…'ceptin' water fer you an' yer horses…There's a trough out to the barn."

"No, ma'am, we're fine, thank you," said Selden.

"What do you want, then?"

"You'd be Thelma Johnson?" asked Jack.

"I am." She wiped the flour on her hands with a dirty dish towel made from a feed sack she was holding.

Is your son, Jessie James, to home?" inquired Selden.

Her face went dark as her eyes squinted at the two lawmen. "Whatchu want him fer?…Lawdogs done kilt my husband, the boy ain't done nothin'."

"Jest like to talk to him. He about?" asked Jack.

"He ain't."

"Know where he is?" added Selden.

She stared at the two men a moment. "Don't…He be out huntin'. We ain't got no meat…Ner much of anythin' else, 'ceptin' some weevily flour an' moldy cornmeal…Tryin' to make us some bread with the flour."

"How long's he been gone?" asked Jack.

Thelma stared at them again for a moment before she answered, "Couple days, reckon."

"Know when he'll be back?" inquired Selden.

She shook her head. "No idee…When he finds some game, reckon."

"He walk huntin'?" continued Lindsey.

"Horsebackin'."

"Yeah…Know what kinda gun he's carryin'?" asked Jack.

They could see her jaw muscles work in the drawn paper-thin skin that covered her face.

"His daddy's buffler gun…Sharps I think it is. All he left us," she said. "He was a buffler hunter till they's all gone…He wuz jest carryin' his old handgun when the laws shot 'im…Fetched him dead, they did."

"Believe he killed a couple folks with that handgun durin' the commission of a stage robbery…The driver an' a passenger, ma'am," said Selden.

"Gotta eat." Was the only thing she said.

Jack touched his hat brim. "Thank you, kindly, Miz Johnson." He reached back to his saddlebags. "Got some extry fatback, beans and cornmeal, if you'd like to have it."

"Don't need ner want no lawdog charity."

Jack nodded and closed the flap on his bags. "Yessum…We'll try back in a few days…Meby your boy will be to home then."

"Suit yerselves," she mumbled as she turned and went back in the house.

MOM TUCKER'S LIVERY
JACKSBORO, TEXAS

"Got everything you need, Pard?" asked Bone as he stepped up into the saddle on Hildebrandt.

"Probably not…but, I'll make do," Loraine replied.

"Ya'll got 'bout two days worth of grain. Your horses shouldn't need mor'n that. There's plenty of good blue stem, buffalo an' gamagrass graze 'tween here an' Bluegrove…Great cattle country," said Mom Tucker. "I checked their shoes, this mornin'…be fine."

"Thanks, Mom, we should make Buffalo Springs by dark, according to the map," added Bone.

"Should…Good place to camp. Plenty water…Smart ya'll changed back into your buckskins an' tied those sheepskin jackets on top of your soogans…Think there's gonna be a frost tonight…Elbows' hurtin' some."

"Joy," said Loraine.

"Just a minute." Mom walked inside the barn.

Loraine arched her well-shaped eyebrows at Bone. He just shrugged.

Mom came back out with a red woolen scarf and handed it to Loraine. "You may need this hon, since you don't wear a hat. Tie this over the top of your head and under your chin…Keep your ears warm."

"Well, thank you, Mom. One of those things I didn't think about."

"Like the privacy paper you didn't think about last time we were on the trail…Gonna miss that undershirt. I liked it."

"Damn you, Bone."

He winked at Mom as they nudged their horses into a smooth amble trot and headed north out of town.

"She's gonna shoot him one of these days," Mom muttered as she pulled out her corncob pipe and doeskin pouch of maple flavored smoking tobacco from her front bib pocket of her overalls.

She packed it, got a match from the small watch

pocket, scratched it across her ample bottom and lit the pipe.

CLAY COUNTY

The sun was settling toward the western horizon, casting a red glow over the grasslands of north Texas. The clear skies and light wind from the north foretold of a coming freeze.

Bone and Loraine approached a tree-shrouded creek in the distance.

"That would be Buffalo Springs, I'll bet," said Bone.

"Hope so. Need to see a man about a dog in the worst way," commented Loraine.

"Got your privacy papers?"

She shook her head and pursed her lips. "Yes, smart ass."

"You sure you know what poison ivy looks like?"

"Nice try, Bone. If you think you're going to go and check out my spot for me...Think again and if you try to use that bracelet of invisibility Lucy gave you...Swear to God, I'll shoot you where you think…and I'm not talking about that big lump sitting on your shoulders."

"Ooo, getting sexy, now, are we?"

"Damn you, Bone."

§§§

CHAPTER NINE

ARBUCKLE MOUNTAINS
CHICKASAW NATION

"Lotta hate in that house," said Jack as he and Selden jogged their mounts back toward Honey Creek.

"Uh-huh...Be interestin' to see if the boy's carryin' it, too."

"Takin' bets?"

Lindsey looked at Jack out from under the wide brim of his black hat. "Not likely."

"When you wanta make another try at catchin' him?" asked Jack.

"Well, if that's him whats been goin' down to Texas an' shootin' those sheriffs and deputies...I'd say let's give him at least another day to git back."

"That'll do."

"I'll call Bone when I git back to Ardmore from that new telephone device in the office now."

"Them things ain't very private, 're they?"

"No, they're not. Got at least six other folks on what the phone company calls a party line...Means any of them others kin listen in to anything I'm sayin'," mulled Selden.

"Don't use no names, then."

"Yep...Good suggestion."

**BUFFALO SPRINGS
CLAY COUNTY**

"You do make good coffee, Pard."

Bone and Loraine sat around the fire enjoying their after dinner Arbuckles, listening to the night sounds of crickets, the few frogs that hadn't gone into hibernation yet, and an occasional owl.

"Thank you, kind sir...That rabbit stew you made was outstanding."

Bone chuckled. "Gotta use something besides my .50 cal next time. Wasn't a whole lot left of the little fellow."

He paused and raised his finger to his lips.

"What?" Loraine mouthed.

Bone pointed off back toward the trail. He cocked his head and listened intently. Then he held up three fingers.

Loraine nodded, changed the hand holding her coffee cup to her left. She slipped her Kimber .45 semiautomatic from the holster and held it alongside her right leg on top of her blanket and ground tarp.

Bone got to his feet, picked up his saddle and soogan and set them out of the light from the fire along with his cup. He then disappeared silently into the dark woods that ran along both sides of the creek.

In a few minutes Loraine also heard the sound of three horses walking toward their fire, their iron shoes clicking on the rocks.

"Hello, the camp," came a voice from the darkness.

"Who is it?" Loraine replied.

"Just a couple of travelers. Smelled yer coffee. Mind if we share some?"

"Just the two of you?" she asked.

"That's it," replied one of the men.

"Come on in, but keep your hands where I can see them," answered Loraine.

The two rough-looking men rode into the camp light, stepped down from their mounts and tied them off at some persimmon saplings nearby.

"Hope you have cups," said Loraine.

"Yessum," said the hawk-faced man. "Always carry a cup."

"Shore do," the second man, a chunky, round-face redheaded individual said, holding up a battered tin cup. "Hey, you be a woman."

"So I'm told," Loraine answered.

"You alone, are ye?" asked hawk face.

"Why are you asking?"

"Oh, jest not safe out here…Nice lookin' woman like yerself…all by your lonesome."

"I think I'll be all right," commented Loraine. "Help yourself to the Arbuckles. Don't mind sharing, but I'm not a waitress."

"Haw, Murf, hear that? She ain't a waitress."

"Yeah, Hawk, she's funny, she is."

"See your name fits," said Loraine.

"Cain't help the way I look. They started callin' me that when I was a little shaver…Reckon it stuck," commented Hawk.

"What are you men doing out this way?" she asked.

"Oh, jest passin' through…Yerself?" said Hawk.

"Same." Loraine took a sip of her coffee.

"Where's yer horse? Didn't see 'im when we rode up," asked Murf.

"She's picketed on some grass down the creek a ways."

Hawk glanced over at the other man. "Well, Murf, since she's out here all by her lonesome. Might as well stay an' keep her company…What say?"

A lecherous grin spread across Murf's face. "Couldn't a said it better my ownself...Don't remember when I had any Mescan meat."

"You boys are making a big mistake...and I mean really big."

"That a fact?" said Hawk, his gapped-tooth, tobacco stained grin matched Murf's.

Loraine smiled, also, but never moved from her spot leaning up against her saddle. Her right hand still held her .45 hidden by her leg. "Carve it in stone, boys, carve it in stone."

"Well, I'll show you somethin' big, sweet thang." He glanced back at his partner. "Keep her covered, Murf...Come on in Rooster," he shouted over his shoulder as he started unbuttoning his dirty canvas trousers.

Murf drew his Remington and pointed it at Loraine. The lecherous sneer got even bigger on his round face. "Be sure to save me some."

Loraine laughed softly as a large bearded man, even more filthy than Hawk and Murf, strolled into camp carrying a '76 Winchester.

"What in hell you laughin' at girlie?" asked Hawk.

"Oh, just how silly you boys are going to look walking into the next town barefoot and wearing just your longjohns."

"Haw, listen to that boys...Here we are with three guns an' you got nothin'," said Rooster before he spat a long stream of viscous tobacco juice at the fire where it popped and sizzled on a burning log. He didn't bother to wipe the spittle from his beard.

Loraine raised her Kimber from alongside her leg and pointed it at the big man with a two-handed grip. "Anybody as ugly as you should know better than to say that."

"Looky there, she's got a toy gun. Funny lookin' thang, ain't it?" said Hawk.

"Plus she's got a friend...and I wouldn't call that a toy," came a deep voice from the darkness that was quickly followed by a giant form appearing at the edge of camp to the right of the three men.

"The hell you say," said Rooster as he started to swing the Winchester in Bone's direction.

The still night air was shattered by a monstrous explosion and a huge ball of fire from the muzzle of Bone's .50 cal, Smith and Wesson 500 handgun. Rooster never had the chance to bring the repeater around into play,

Shattered pieces of the '76 Winchester went in all directions as what was left of the rifle spun out of Rooster's massive hands and splattered his face and chest with blood.

The big bearded man screamed like a woman as he sunk to his knees holding what was left of his right hand, trying to stop the bleeding.

Loraine snapped off two rounds that sounded like one shot, sending the hats of Hawk and Murf flying back behind them. Hawk's was a gray slouch hat and Murf's was a battered, tall chocolate bowler.

Blood trickled down Hawk's stunned face from a shallow groove along the top of his head beginning at his hairline.

Murf looked down at the yellow puddle gathering around his worn Thomas Jefferson brogans. "My Gawd in Heaven," he whispered as he reached up and felt the top of his head.

"My hand, my hand," cried Rooster as he rocked back and forth on his knees in pain. "Somebody please help me."

Hawk pulled his bandana from about his neck and held it on the bloody crease through his greasy dark brown hair. "Who the hell are you?" He looked first at Loraine and then at Bone.

"You don't really want to know, slick nickel…You don't really want to know," said Bone, with his enigmatic grin.

Hawk glanced back to Loraine. "Ya'll married er somethin'?"

She chuckled. "Not in this lifetime, asswipe…Now, unbuckle those gunbelts and start peeling those boots and clothes off…down to your drawers."

"Huh?"

"You heard me. I've already told you once, you scum were going to look funny walking into the next town barefooted and in your longjohns…Not going to say it again."

"I think she said 'silly' earlier, Hawk," said Murf.

"What?" Hawk responded.

"Either or, your choice," said Bone. "Just get it done…Now." He thumbed the hammer back on his 500, the double clicks made ominous sounds in the quietness.

"Awright, awright. Jest don't shoot that dang hand cannon no more," said Hawk.

Ken Farmer

"Anybody gonna help me 'fore I bleed plumb to death?" whined Rooster.

"You're too ugly to bleed to death...Lord, you ever look in a mirror."

"I'm dying here an' she's a pickin' on me," said Rooster.

"Believe me, jackwagon, if she wanted to pick on you, you could tell the difference. Now shed those duds. We'll wrap your hand in your shirt...Get it off," ordered Bone, waving the .50 cal back toward him. "Ya'll pile your weapons over there next to the firepit."

"I'm goin', I'm goin'...Ain't this agin' the law?" asked Rooster.

"Just call it Bone's Law, maggot," said Bone.

"What's Bone's Law?"

"Mine," he answered and grinned again.

The three ne'er-do-wells peeled down to their ragged union suits. Murf wrapped Rooster's mangled hand, now missing three fingers, in his filthy shirt.

"Say, ain't that shirt too dirty to be a wrappin' my shot up hand in?"

"Now, whose fault is that?" asked Loraine.

"Take off, boys," said Bone as he waved the muzzle of the giant handgun in the direction of the creek.

"But, that's the creek...We'll git wet," complained Murf.

"From the way you boys smell, it'll do you some good. That's the general direction to the closest town," said Bone.

"What about our horses?" asked Hawk.

"What horses?" asked Loraine.

"The horses we tied up over...Oh...right," commented Hawk.

"This ain't nice, you know," grumbled Murf.

"You got a lot of gall, scumbag, considering what you intended to do with my partner there." Bone nodded at Loraine.

"How about we just shoot them, Bone?...We haven't shot anybody today...yet." she said as she raised her Kimber with both hands, took a modified Weaver stance and aimed it at Rooster.

"Now, wait a minute...wait a minute," stammered the big, bearded man as he backed away and held his good hand up.

"Then we'd have to bury them, Pard."

"Oh…Didn't think about that," Loraine replied as she lowered her weapon.

The three men hobbled off to the creek as fast as they could, barefoot, and waded across. The trap door on Rooster's union suit only had one button.

"Dangomighty, this is cold," said Murphy.

On the other side, they headed east toward the small farming community of Vashti.

Loraine turned to Bone as the bad guys disappeared into the darkness. "How did you know they were coming?"

"Oh, just something Bass Reeves taught me…Listen for what shouldn't be there."

§§§

CHAPTER TEN

MCGANN CABIN
ARBUCKLE MOUNTAINS

It was well past dark-thirty when Jack and Selden pulled rein at the large red barn next to the log house the McGann's called home. Doctor Winchester Ashalatubbi's buggy still sat at the side of the barn with his sorrel mare munching on a flake of alfalfa in the paddock.

"Looks like *Anompoli Lawa* decided to stay overnight again…You just as well spend the night, too, Sel. Way too late to ride back to Ardmore," said Jack.

"Was thinkin' the same thing, myself."

He and Jack stepped down and were promptly greeted by Son and Bear.

"Durn, almost cain't see Bear in the dark," said Selden of the black wolf.

"Yeah, I know…But, in the light, they're like salt and pepper. Both have golden eyes, though. The Chickasaw say it's a link to the spirits," replied Jack.

"It is true," came a voice from the darkness near the house.

Jack lit a coal oil lantern left hanging on the gate post at the corral by his wife, Angie, and turned up the wick so they could see to strip the tack from their mounts.

The two lawmen turned to see the venerable white-haired Chickasaw Shaman, *Anompoli Lawa*, whose Christian name was Winchester Ashalatubbi.

He was also the medical doctor for the tribe with his office in Ardmore.

"*Sheeah, Anompoli Lawa*," said Marshal Lindsey.

"*Sheeah*, Selden Lindsey," Doctor Ashalatubbi responded with the Chickasaw greeting as he walked closer. "We do believe a golden-eyed wolf is a link to the spirit world and works at the direction of *Chí-hóo-wah*, the Great Spirit."

"If you say so, Doc. Would never disagree with any explanation you give about the spirits or God…Still amazes me that the Indian name for God is *Chí-hóo-wah*…Sounds so much like *Jehovah* from the Bible, it's spooky," said Selden.

The Shaman smiled. "There is only one God and we all worship him…We have used *Chí-hóo-wah* for a thousand years…long before the white man set foot on this continent. You are familiar with the lost tribe of Israel?"

"Heard my grandma talk about them. She knew the Bible backwards an' forward…Are you sayin' the lost tribe of Israel came to America?"

"I can only say what I know about some of our words that have Hebrew links…You know about the ancient petroglyphs in the cave behind Turner Falls?"

"I saw them when I was shot an' washed over the falls an' managed to crawl up in that cave...Where Angie found me," said Jack.

Lindsey nodded. "Yeah, seen 'em, too. Don't know what they are, though."

"One of them appears to be a *Menorah*..."

Marshal Lindsey interrupted him. "What's a *Men-orah*?"

"It's a seven-branched candelabrum, world's oldest continuously used religious symbol by the Jewish people...Well over two thousand years old...Having been a student of divinity and studying Hebrew, I recognized several particular petroglyphs as also being in the Masoretic Text. They illustrate...*Jehovah - God of Israel*."

"You're not kiddin', are you?"

"I am not, Marshal...Some think that when the Temple of Solomon was destroyed by Nebuchadnezzar II in 587 BC, one of the tribes of Israel somehow made it across the Atlantic to America...and apparently some came all the way to the Arbuckles...Just supposition on my part, you understand."

"Great guns…"

"Not keepin' the supper warm all night, so if the two of ye be wantin' to eat, best ye quit palaverin' with me uncle an' come inside," interrupted Angie from the porch.

"Don't have to tell me twice," said Jack as he turned and headed toward the house. "So you decided to stay another night, did you, Uncle?"

"It would appear so, Jack. Aurali Red asked me to tell her and Baby Sarah some *Bible* stories and I guess we lost track of time. Next thing we knew, it was evening and Angie had set supper on the table."

"Those girls can get their way without you even knowing that they 're doin' it," Jack said as he opened the door to the house. "Angie's teachin' 'em early."

"Angie's teachin' who, what, early?"

"Oh, uh…Teaching the girls, uh…how to cook, dear. How to cook," stammered Jack.

"Uh-huh…an' I think ye're full of the blarney, Marmaduke Jackson McGann."

"Marmaduke? Haw," exclaimed Selden.

"Selden Trullery Lindsey…Haw, back," said Jack as he thrust his lower jaw forward.

"That's enough, you two. It's best ye be sittin' down before I throw it to the hogs," chastised Angie.

WILSON RANCH
COOKE COUNTY, TEXAS

"Wonder how Bone an' Loraine are comin' along huntin' for that sniper?" asked Mason as he took a sip of his after dinner coffee.

He, Fiona, Mary Lou, Lucy and Cletus sat in the large living room located on the west side of the twelve foot wide dog run that went from the front door to the screen-in back porch. The overly large hallway also served as a parlor, with couches and chairs along the wall.

There was a crackling fire in the native stone fireplace in the living area to cut the chill of the evening.

"They sent a telegram to Jack and Selden for them to go see the Johnsons," said Lucy.

"See, I told that's what they would do, husband."

"That's amazin' you can do that, Lucy," said Mason.

"Do what?"

"Know what Bone an' Loraine are doin'."

She laughed. "I told you that he is an especially strong sender…and actually he got that ability from the combination of your and Fiona's genes. You two also are senders and receivers…just not to the degree he is."

"Where are they now?" asked Fiona.

"They're camped at a place called Buffalo Springs, on the way up to see the Cobb family. They had to discipline three ne'er-do-wells that thought they could have their way with Loraine…She and Bone pretended she was on the trail alone when the three men approached last night." Lucy giggled.

"Uh-oh…You have to tell us what they did," said Mason.

"Needless to say, the three men didn't have much of a chance. One of them is minus three fingers that were on the hand holding his rifle… curtesy of Bone's big handgun…and the other two lost their hats when Loraine shot them off with hers."

"Let me guess…then they made the bad guys

walk to town in their underwear...barefoot," offered Fiona with a big smile.

Lucy grinned back at her and nodded. "Exactly."

"He and Loraine are my kind of law officers," said Mason, also smiling.

BUFFALO SPRINGS

"What are we going to do with those horses and guns?" Loraine asked as she scraped some beans and salt pork into Bone's blue swirl agateware plate.

"Well, I'd say we daisy chain them and take them with us...along with the guns. Think we can leave the clothes here." He set his plate on a rock, blew across his cup and took a sip of the stout trail brew Loraine had made when she got up at sunrise.

"Is that legal?"

"What? Leaving their clothes here?"

"Damn you, Bone. You know what I mean."

He chuckled. "Perks of the trade in this day and time, Pard, perks of the trade...Like those bounties we collected on Wild Bob's gang."

"Good point...Glad you said we'd leave the clothes here. I don't even want to pick them up and throw them in the fire...Did you get a whiff of them?" Loraine said as she filled her own plate.

"Yeah, that's why I moved them downwind with that long branch...Let's eat up, Pard, and hit the trail before the wind shifts and the frost starts to thaw." He picked up a crispy piece of salt pork and took a big bite.

"Sometimes you actually make sense, Bone," said Loraine.

Thirty minutes later they were amble trotting along the ranch road heading toward the Cobb farm. The sun was just above the tree line, its early morning rays created a light ground fog from the frosty ground.

Bone led two of the confiscated horses and Loraine one. The guns and gunbelts were looped over the saddlehorns.

"How much further do you think?" asked Loraine.

"Well, by dead reckoning, Pard, we're about five miles out of Bluegrove. I hope we come across a native, maybe they can tell us where the Cobb place is."

"Looks like a wagon coming this way. Here's your chance," she said.

Bone held up his hand as the buckboard with a grizzled farmer in the middle of the seat rolled up.

"How do? Hep ye?" said the fifty something farmer as he spat a stream of amber tobacco juice off to the side of the road and pulled back on the leathers. "Damn," he said as he wiped the excess spittle from the stubble on his chin with his sleeve.

"I'm Deputy Bone and this is Deputy Rodriguez. We're looking for the Cobb place. Do you happen to know Cherokee and June?"

He studied Bone and Loraine for a long moment and then asked, "What's he done now?" He spat again. "Damn." He wiped his chin once more.

"Nothing that we know of...Just like to talk to him."

The farmer studied them again and then focused on the spare horses. "Go back down this road 'bout 'nother mile...You'll see a bodark tree, got a bunch of horse apples on it. Turn left there down that wagon trail...Now if'n you come to a two foot wet-weather branch, you done gone too far. Gotta turn around an' go back to that tree...Where'd you git them horses? Look like the Smart brother's nags."

"That their name?" asked Loraine.

"Yeppers, Japeth's the oldest. Likes to call his self Rooster...The other two brothers is Rufus an' Meshack...Rufus goes by Hawk, don't need no explainin', an' Meshack goes by Murf, on account he cain't pronounce Meshack...Worthless bunch, ever was one, ask me."

"Well, don't think they lived up to their name. Tried to harass Deputy Rodriguez here because she's a woman...Rooster is minus three fingers and they're all minus clothes and boots while they walk toward Vashti."

The farmer jerked off his battered old fedora and slapped his thigh with it. "Hotdamno'mighty! He-he-he, that's the funniest thang I heard in a month of Sundays...Oh!" He coughed and gagged a little. "Dangnation, swallered my chaw...But, nonevermind...Thankee, Deputies, you done my old heart good...Cain't wait to tell the spit'n whittle boys down to the feed store...He, he, he."

"Had trouble with the Smarts before?" asked Loraine.

"Could say…Yep, they's jest a bunch of wannabe road agents an' bullies."

"You don't say?" replied Bone.

"Jest did…Them three's useless as tits on a boar hog."

"I can believe it," said Loraine, stifling a giggle.

"He-he-he…Come up there, Bill." He flicked the reins over the rump of the spavined old bay gelding pulling his wagon. "He-he-he."

Bone and Loraine glanced back over their shoulders as the wagon clattered on down the rutted road—the farmer still cackling.

"Well, we must have done something right, Pard."

Loraine grinned. "You think?"

Bone's face showed his enigmatic smile. "Let's hope our next stop is as equally productive."

§§§

CHAPTER ELEVEN

CLAY COUNTY

Bone and Loraine slowed their horses to a walk as they came into sight of the Cobb home.

"Expecting trouble?" asked Loraine.

"Can't always tell, Pard. Best to be prepared, don't you think?"

"In this case…I'd say yes."

They reined up about ten yards from the rusty tin roofed, clapboard house that was badly in need of repair and a good whitewashing.

"Hello, the house," shouted Bone.

He and Loraine exchanged glances.

"Hello, the house," he yelled again.

A ten year old waif with long stringy brown hair, wearing a worn, thin, red and blue patterned cotton flour sack dress came from around the side of the house.

"Hi," said Loraine. "Are you Susan?"

"Uh-huh. Who are you?"

"I'm Loraine and this is Bone. Are your mommy and daddy around?"

"Daddy's down to the garden by the crick an' momma's inside…She's feelin' some porely…Got the croup."

"Well, why don't you point us in the direction of your garden…Don't need to bother your mom if she's not feeling well," said Bone.

Susan stepped forward and pointed off to her right toward a line of trees. "He be down there on the other side of that crick."

"Thanks, honey," said Loraine as she followed Bone and Hildebrandt toward the tree line a little over fifty yards away.

They followed a path that led through the woods to the shallow creek and waded their horses across. At the edge of the tree line, they stopped, tied their mounts and the confiscated horses to a couple of saplings and loosened their girths.

They could see a forty something man in faded blue bib overalls, an equally faded denim shirt and a worn and sweat-stained old cavalry slouch hat, out in the two acre garden. He had a bushel basket he carried along the row of stunted corn as he pulled the dried ears.

"We'll show our gold detective shields from the department, Pard, since we don't have any deputy marshal badges."

"Yeah, maybe he won't look too close to the lettering on them."

"Worth a shot...Howdy," yelled Bone from the edge of the field.

The man looked up, took his hat off, wiped his brow with a worn red paisley bandana and walked in their direction.

"How do. What kin I do fer you?"

"I take it you're Cherokee Cobb?" said Bone.

"You take purty good, big man. You have me at a disadvantage…I don't know who you are."

"I'm Deputy US Marshal Bone and this is Deputy US Marshal Rodriguez. Do you have a moment?"

He and Loraine flashed their heavy cast brass badges from 2018 that they normally wore attached to their belts or hung on a chain around their necks.

Cobb only glanced at the badges. "Reckon so. You bein' the law an' all. Just tryin' to get what little truck we got 'fore a freeze gits 'em…Let's step over yonder to the trees. Got a jug of water in the shade of that red oak."

The three walked over to the tree where Cobb picked up his quart Mason jar, next to his rifle that was leaning against the oak, unscrewed the lid and offered it to Loraine.

"No, thanks," she said.

"We're good," added Bone.

Cherokee took a long drink and put the lid back on the jar and set it back in the grass where it was.

"Now, what can I do for ya'll?"

"Nice rifle…Sharps-Borchardt?" asked Bone.

"Uh-huh, '78...Wuz in the cavalry durin' the Injun wars...Company Marksman. Let me keep it...Before the laws sent me to Huntsville."

"Understand you and your brother held up a mercantile...customer was killed," said Loraine.

"He drew down on us...Didn't have no choice."

"Yes, you did...You could have not held up the store in the first place," Loraine responded.

"Couldn't get a job when I got out of the cavalry...needed the money." He looked down at his feet. "Kilt my baby brother when the posse chased us down."

"Should have just given yourselves up," Loraine added.

"Shoulda done a lot of things, reckon...but didn't. Was kindly desperate...I done my time." He took a deep breath. "June an' my baby suffered mor'n I done."

Bone nodded. "Been doing any traveling?"

He looked the big man in the eye. "Not so's you'd notice...Town an' so forth, you know, gittin' supplies an' sellin' what vegetables we don't need."

"Recently?" he asked.

"Couple days ago...Why?"

"Been to Wise County?" asked Bone.

Cobb stared first at Bone, and then at Loraine. "What's this all about?"

"The men in the posse that tracked you and your brother down are being killed...one by one," said Loraine.

"An' you think I'm a doin' it?" questioned Cobb as he ground his teeth, flexing his jaw muscles.

"Didn't say that. We're just talking to everybody that posse arrested back in the day that's still around," commented Bone.

"Well it ain't me," Cobb said with anger rising in his voice. "Think we're done here...Got work to do. My wife's sick an' I cain't afford fer the doc to come out...an' my Susie's hungry all the time...Ya'll need to git off my property."

He stared at Bone without blinking, and then turned and headed back out to his garden.

Bone and Loraine exchanged glances.

"I take it that the interview is over," said Loraine as she watched Cobb start striping corn from the stalks again.

"You think?" commented Bone as he walked over to their horses, snugged up his cinch and mounted Hildebrandt.

Loraine followed his lead, and then stepped up on Sweet Face. "Think we've got work to do. Need to go check out the widow Waverly and eliminate her from the list." She shifted her weight to the right to re-center the saddle. "Don't think there's much of a chance she's the one, do you?"

"She's seventy years old, Pard. What do you think?"

"Point...Still have to interview her."

"We do, but seventy is older'n dirt in this time."

They crossed back over the creek with the Smart brother's mounts and trotted toward the narrow road.

"That rifle of his is the long range model. It's a hammerless, falling block type...Built around 22,000 of them. Shoots a .45-70 round. Very accurate...Effective at over 500 yards, with a max range of over 1,000 yards," said Bone looking at Loraine.

"Sounds perfect for what's been happening and I would say...he could have revenge on his mind," she commented, glancing back at her partner.

"You think?" retorted Bone, repeating what he said earlier. "There was a lot of pain in those eyes."

WILSON RANCH

"Anything new, Lucy?" asked Flynn as he and Fiona sat out on the porch in rocking chairs.

She nodded. "They just left the Cobb place." Lucy spent the next ten minutes bringing Mason and Fiona up to date on the meeting with Cherokee Cobb.

"...and that's pretty much it. He and Loraine have moved Cobb up to a suspect from a person of interest...were Bone's thoughts," said Lucy.

Mason nodded. "Just the fact of him having that long range buffalo gun certainly puts him in the middle of the bulls eye, alright."

Fiona agreed, "With his wife being sick and daughter not getting enough nourishment on top of your posse killing his brother..."

"Didn't really have any choice, hon. Tracked them to an old hunter's cabin up on the Red...Ordered them to come out with their hands up an' Billy Cobb burst out the front door with a pistol in each hand, firing as fast as he could cock the hammer an' pull the triggers." Mason paused.

"Did any of the posse get hit?" asked Fiona.

He shook his head. "No...Reckon it was me that put him down 'fore any of our posse did take one of his bullets...He wasn't...wasn't but fifteen, Fiona...He wasn't but fifteen..." Mason took a deep breath and stared off in the distance. "That's...that's one that never goes away." He pursed his lips as he fought back the tears.

Lucy got up from her spot on the stoop and walked over to Flynn and hugged him around the neck. "You didn't have a choice, Mason," she whispered.

He nodded. "Doesn't make his face go away though...He wasn't even shavin' yet."

JACK COUNTY

"If we push it, we should make Jacksboro a little after dark," said Bone.

"If it means not having to sleep on the ground again...Let's do it," replied Loraine.

"I know Hildebrandt can make it without flagging, what about Sweet Face?"

"She got a good rest last night, there was plenty of grass, too. If we keep them at an amble, she should be all right. If she starts to lather and labor at all, we'll have to stop."

"We'll stop and let them blow every five miles or so anyway…Don't believe in stressing them."

"Me neither. Gotten kind of attached to her already."

"Yeah, know what you mean…If it was just your bubble butt getting tired, we'd go on…"

"Damn you, Bone," Loraine snapped at him. "I don't have a bubble butt."

"Nothing wrong with a bubble butt, Pard…Actually, I kind of like 'em." He got his enigmatic grin across his face.

"Your time's coming, big boy, your time's coming."

Bone chuckled. "Promises, promises, that's all I ever get."

Fifteen miles later they were in Jack County, Bone and Loraine had stopped to rest the horses at the side of the semi-wooded road and had just remounted. The afternoon was alive with nature's cacophony of sounds, including two Bobwhite quail calling to each other with their distinctive two beat whistles that gave them their name.

"Hear that?"

"Yeah, what are they?" asked Loraine.

"Bobwhite quail. Live on the ground in the brush...Almost gone in our time. They are saying, Bob-White...Bob-White."

"Oh, it does sound that way, doesn't it?"

"It's what the captain and I were hunting when we met Lucy in 2014."

"Thought you said they were almost gone?"

"Did. But they have a hunting season for them to help manage their population with the shrinking of their habitat."

"I'll never understand that," she replied.

"There's only so much land for them to live on, Pard, with all the expansion of housing developments in rural areas...Only so much food."

"Oh, I see...Makes sense," she said as the two birds repeated their Bob-Whites to each other.

"Making good time, Pard. We should..."

He was interrupted by a shot from up ahead on the other side of a small rise.

"Oh, damn, that was a handgun, wasn't it?" asked Loraine.

"It was. Come on…leave the other horses." Bone clucked and bumped Hildebrandt into a gallop with his Apache style knee-high moccasin clad heels.

They rounded a curve in the road and topped the hill to see a six-up Concord stage stopped in the middle of the road. There were four masked men on horseback. Two on each side of the coach.

They heard one of the men yell, "Stand an' deliver or suffer yer death!"

"Spread out, Pard," he shouted at her just behind him over his shoulder. "Shoot over their heads…It's just like those mounted shooting contests we do back home."

"I know…But, these balloons are armed." Loraine swerved Sweet Face off to the right and drew her Kimber.

"And we're using real ammo instead of crushed walnut shell blanks, too…It's their funeral. Oorah!"

Loraine and Bone kicked their mounts into an all-out hard gallop.

BONE'S LAW

The four highway men turned at the sound of Bone and Loraine's horses pounding hooves on the hard dirt road and started firing at them with their handguns.

Bone had his S & W 500 in his hand. He held it straight out in front of his shoulder. "Do it, Pard," he yelled.

Her .45 semiautomatic barked at the two robbers on her side. They continued their fire back.

Bone's hand cannon boomed at the other two as he and Loraine charged full tilt at them.

The outlaw closest to the stage took one of the big rounds from Bone to the center of his chest, flipped over backward out of his saddle and landed three feet behind his horse. He was dead when he hit the ground.

Both highway men on Loraine's side were also knocked from their saddles with her first three shots.

The remaining robber on Bone's side threw down his weapon and held both hands in the air. "I give...I give. Don't shoot no more," he yelled as Hildebrandt slid to a stop in front of him.

"Out of that saddle, scumbag. On your face and eat dirt. Hands behind your head...Now! Do it now!" Bone ordered, thumbing the hammer back on his big .50 cal. for added effect, even though it was a double-action pistol.

The road agent quickly did as he was told.

Bone glanced over at Loraine. "Get yours, Pard?" he asked.

She looked back at him, gave him a nod, and then sagged to the left and slowly slid out of her saddle, like cold molasses, to the ground…

§§§

CHAPTER TWELVE

WILSON RANCH

Lucy sat bolt upright from the day bed on the screened-in back porch where she was taking an afternoon nap. She jumped up and ran barefoot down the wide dog run hallway to the wraparound front porch.

Mason and Fiona sat in slatback, calf hide bottom rockers and were talking with Cletus and Mary Lou. All four were nursing cups of coffee.

Lucy burst through the green gingerbread screen door and clamored, "Mason, Fiona...I must go to Jacksboro...Quickly,"

"What is it?" asked Fiona.

"Loraine's been shot!"

"The sniper?" asked Mason, as he jumped to his feet.

She shook her head. "No, she and Bone stopped a stagecoach robbery north of Jacksboro...We must go."

"Better go by horseback instead of the buggy...make better time." Mason looked at Fiona. "And you're not going, my love."

"Don't tell me..."

Mason drew to his full six feet and two inches and looked at his wife—his sky-blue eyes, didn't blink. "We're going to have to do some hard riding...It is not open to discussion, period."

Fiona cocked her head, and then grinned. "Yes, husband...but, let Lucy ride Spot. He'll take care of her."

Mason embraced Fiona and held her to his body for a moment, and then leaned back and kissed her sweetly. "I love you Fiona Mae Flynn...Don't ever forget that."

"I know you do and I love you, too, Mason Reese Flynn...with all my heart."

They kissed again.

"Cletus, help me saddle the boys?" asked Flynn as they broke apart.

His brother-in-law nodded, led the way down the steps and toward the barn.

"Lucy put what ever you need in a carpet bag...Take some warm clothes, we may get another cold front...It's that time of year."

"I will," Lucy replied to Mason as she opened the screen door and went back inside the house.

"Fiona and I will go pack ya'll some supplies for the trail. You'll never make Jacksboro before nightfall," said Mary Lou.

"Thanks, Sis," yelled Mason over his shoulder.

In less than fifteen minutes, Mason and Lucy had said their good byes and headed down the ranch road at a trot. Spot was in his natural single foot and Sailor was in a road amble.

They were traveling at around ten miles an hour and would only need to slow to a walk every five miles or so.

"At this speed, we should make Alvord in Wise County by dark. Won't have to sleep on the ground...Got a nice hotel there," said Flynn. "And some really good restaurants."

"I don't mind, Mason," commented Lucy.

"We have to go right through there anyway...It's on a straight shot to Jacksboro."

"Too bad we can't travel at night."

"Road's too rough...rutted an' all. One or both of our horses could bow a tendon, or worse...in the dark."

"I understand," said Lucy. "We just need to get there as soon as possible."

JACK COUNTY

"Loraine!" Bone shouted as he jumped down from Hildebrandt and ran around to the near side of the coach.

Some of the passengers were exiting the stage. Bone had dropped his reins to the ground when he sprinted around to Loraine's side. A rancher knew to grab the reins before the big, sable horse spooked.

Bone slid to his knees at Loraine's limp form and cradled her up in his arms. He could see the blood begin to stain her buckskin top from a pencil-sized hole just above her right breast.

"Anybody got a handkerchief or any kind of cloth?" he asked of the passengers stepping out of that side of the coach.

"Hang in there, Loraine, just hang in there." Bone held her tight and then looked up as a garishly dressed drummer handed him his handkerchief from an inside coat pocket.

"Here, it's clean."

"Thanks," Bone said as he took the cloth and stuffed it inside her top directly on the bleeding wound in her upper chest.

"Can I be of any help?" asked a woman passenger.

Bone pulled Loraine to his chest. "Is there any blood on her back?"

"Yes, and a hole just above her shoulder blade."

He nodded. "I need another cloth."

The woman lifted her ankle length gray twill wool travel dress, tore a long strip from one of her white cotton petticoats and folded it into a pad.

She knelt down beside them, lifted the soft leather collar of Loraine's top and placed the pad on top of the quarter-size exit wound in her back.

"Thank you," Bone said as he got to his feet with Loraine cradled in his arms like she was no more than a child. "Stay with me, Loraine, you hear me? Stay with me," he whispered to the side of her face.

Loraine's eyes fluttered as she looked up into Bone's face, just inches from her own. "Damn you, Bone, what makes you think I'm...I'm going any...where." She leaned her head against his broad chest.

"I can't lose you, Loraine...I can't," his voice broke as he whispered to her. "You gotta stay with me...You hear me?"

She blinked again and looked up into his gold-flecked brown eyes that were beginning to fill. "This is the first time you ever called me Loraine, you big lug...Are you crying?"

"No...no, course not. Just got dust in 'em when we were riding up, shooting at the bad guys."

Loraine laid her head back down on his chest. "Liar." She passed out.

Bone carried her to the coach door as if she weighed no more than a baby. He looked up at the driver and messenger. "How far is Jacksboro?...We're Jack County deputy sheriffs."

"Slap Aint Gussie Nell in the face! Yer them same two what stopped Wild Bob an' his gang when we wuz on the Fort Worth run...Man mountain Bone with his hand cannon an' his lady partner, Loraine...Hoo-law dang!" He slapped the shoulder of the guard next to him. "Doin' the Henrietta to Jacksboro today. I'm Charlie Mitchell an' this here's Pearly Clark...'member us?" He nodded at the shotgun messenger.

"I do...Now, how far to Jacksboro?"

"Wellsir, we kin only make 'bout five miles a hour, so gonna take least five, meby six hours...Got no station 'tween here an' there, so gotta baby the boys here."

"Can you load these miscreants on top? I got shackles for the survivor on the ground on the other side."

"Shore, Deputy Bone...Tie yer mounts to the back, too."

"Let's do it. Need to get my partner to Doc Mosier."

Charlie glanced down on the off side at the outlaw on the ground. The rancher who had grabbed Hildebrandt's reins when Bone dismounted, had his foot on the back of the robber's neck, making sure he didn't get up.

The driver stepped down on the wheel and then to the ground, took the reins to Bone's horse from the rancher and led him to the rear of the coach to tie him off with the attached lead rope.

"Where those shackles?" asked Pearly, the messenger.

"In my pouch here on my side."

Pearly climbed down on the near side, got the shackles from Bone's parfleche and carried them around to the off side.

"Put them hands behind yer back, nabob, 'fore I have that feller with his foot on yer neck to jump up an' down couple times."

"Awright, awright," he quickly said as his words stirred up small clouds of dust from the road, and did as he was bid.

Pearly snapped the heavy cuffs around the man's wrists, nodded at the rancher to remove his foot, and jerked him to his feet. "Now climb up on top of that stage."

"How'm I gonna do that with my hands behind my back?"

"Better figger it out, lest you want me to tie you behind the coach with the horses, an' let you run all the way to Jacksboro...Yer choice, don't matter none to me."

The highwayman grumbled as he put a foot up on the hub of the front wheel, lunged up and hooked his chin on the edge of the box. He wormed his way up and fell over into the boot, landing on the strong box. The man got to his knees, worked his way into the seat, and then rolled over to the top of the coach where he collapsed, exhausted.

Pearly walked back around to the near side of the stage, got Loraine's mare and led her to the rear to tie off.

He and the rancher went to each of the road agent's horses, stripped their tack and swatted them on their rumps.

"No way to trail 'em all the way to Jacksboro," said Pearly. "As I see it...I mind somebody'll pick 'em up," said Pearly.

The rancher nodded. "Yeah, they can fend for themselves long as they don't have saddles and bridles on 'em."

Bone, still cradling Loraine in his arms, glanced down at the wound in her chest and saw traces of a red foam gathering around the hole in her buckskin top from under the pad, and then some bloody bubbles at her lips. "Oh, damn."

Loraine's normally smooth olive skin was a pasty white and her breathing had become very shallow and irregular.

He turned to the woman who had given him part of her petticoat. "Open this door, please, Ma'am."

She stepped over, unlatched the door on the near side of the coach and guided Loraine's legs past the edge as Bone stepped up inside.

"Thank you, Ma'am," he said as he bent over, turned and sat down on the forward facing seat, holding Loraine in his lap.

Bone turned to the outside window. "Charlie, would you get our saddlebags and coats from our mounts?"

"Shore, Deputy."

Bone turned back to Loraine and mused. *Lucy said I could do this…gotta try…gotta try.* He pulled

Loraine to his chest with her cheek against his and closed his eyes.

In a moment, a very soft, almost indiscernible pale blue glow surrounded them and seemed to emanate from between their bodies as her breath became more ragged.

"Come on, Baby, please...please. Don't leave me. Come on, breathe. Please, Honey," he whispered to the side of her face as he caressed it with his free hand, pushed the hair from her eyes, and then looked up. "Please dear God, help me...I never talked to you before, Lord, never asked for anything...but, I'm asking now...Please give me strength...Help me. Don't let her die...Please."

He lowered his head back down. Droplets of sweat beaded up on his forehead as his concentration increased and tears ran down his face and onto hers.

WISE COUNTY, TEXAS

Mason glanced over at Lucy and noticed she was almost catatonic, sitting in the saddle, staring off into space, but seeing nothing. He slowed Sailor to a walk and Spot followed suit.

He started to ask her what the matter was, but something in the back of his mind told him not to—she was all right. Lucy was in full link with Bone...

§§§

CHAPTER THIRTEEN

JACK COUNTY

"Awright we leave now, Deputy Bone?" asked Charlie. "Deputy Rodriguez doin' 'ny better?"

Bone shook off the trance, looked up a little disoriented, and finally figured out where he was as the blue glow subsided. He glanced down at Loraine. She was breathing better.

Bone nodded at Charlie. "Yeah, take off, Charlie. I'll hold her."

"All the way?...Five hours?"

He nodded again. "Doesn't matter how long."

"Awrighty, we got the bodies an' the live one loaded up on top, 'long with their weapons in the rear boot. Yer horses 're tied to the back."

"Appreciate it," he said as the passengers boarded.

The woman who had assisted him earlier sat next to him. The rancher, drummer and a business man sat in the rear facing seat.

"Anything I can do?"

"Yes, Ma'am, looks like I'm going to need a couple of fresh pads...These are saturated."

"I knew there was a reason for all these petticoats," the woman said as she tore two more long strips, folded them into pads and handed him one. She replaced the one on Loraine's back, tore another and wrapped it around her to hold the pads on the wounds. "Looks like the bleeding has almost stopped."

"Thank, God."

"Would you like me to pray for her, too? I heard you praying while ago, before we boarded."

"Yes, Ma'am, I would really appreciate it." He caressed Loraine's face again.

"Come up there boys...H'yah," Charlie yelled from the top of the stage as he slapped the reins over their rumps. He popped his coach whip above their backs without touching them to get them going.

The stage lurched forward as the six horses dug in and overcame the inertia of the heavy load, and then settled into a medium road trot.

Bone held Loraine to his chest, absorbing the jostling of the coach with his own body as much as he could. The thick rubber straps underneath the carriage only partially dampened the rough places in the rutted road.

"Hang in there, Baby, I've got you," he whispered to the side of her face.

He lifted his head up to look down at her and noticed she was still pale. Some of her color had returned and there were no more bubbles on her lips or foam around the wounds. Her breathing became more regular, shallow, but regular.

"Ma'am, would you help me massage her hands? It will help stimulate her circulation."

"Of course," she said, picking up one of Loraine's hands and started rubbing and patting it.

WISE COUNTY

Flynn glanced over at Lucy just as she slumped forward and fell to her left. He quickly side-passed Sailor to catch the diminutive alien, pull her to his saddle in front of him, and reined the line-back grulla gelding to a halt. Spot stopped also.

He stepped down from the saddle and carried Lucy over to a large rock on the side of the road and sat down. She began to stir and opened her eyes.

"Mason, I need some water, please," Lucy said as she took several deep breaths.

"Can you sit up?" he asked.

She nodded.

Flynn got to his feet, turned, set her on top of the rock, walked over to Sailor and retrieved his leather covered canteen. He carried it back, unscrewed the top and handed it to her.

Lucy took a long draught of the tepid well water, rested a moment, and then took another. When she finished, she smiled and handed the canteen back to Mason. "Thank you, so much."

"You were in contact with Bone, weren't you?"

"Yes, he was trying to use the transfer of life energy on Loraine and needed my help."

"Guess I'll never understand that and you've done it to me."

"It's just something we learned to control millennia ago…Like Bone, it's strong in you and Fiona…not as much as in him, but, it's there, none the less…This was the first time I've ever done it or helped do it remotely. It does require a physical touch."

"Is Loraine going to be all right?" asked Mason.

"She's better and out of immediate danger, but she'll need more direct attention." Lucy paused and took several more deep breaths. "Bone and I together were able to stop the internal bleeding and seal off her punctured lung…Your Doctor Mosier will still have to put stitches in the large exit wound…She's not quite in the clear yet."

JACK COUNTY

"Does anyone have any water?" asked Bone.

"I do, Deputy," said the rancher as he bent over and retrieved a canteen from the floor between his feet and handed it to Bone.

"Appreciate it." He took several long drinks and handed it back to the rancher.

"May I ask you a question, Deputy?" asked the woman.

"Certainly. Not sure I'll be able to answer it, though. But, go ahead."

"What was that blue haze that seemed to be around you and her when we boarded?"

Bone grinned. "Madam, I wish I knew. All I know is that she was dying and I had to give her some of my spirit or soul, if you will...I'm not aware of the blue haze, as you call it...It's something I learned from a...uh...Shaman."

"I saw it too...It was almost like a very thin fog," added the rancher.

"Huh? I wouldn't..." Bone glanced down at Loraine's face.

Her eyes flickered as she looked up at his face and took a breath. "Bone, what happened?"

"You got shot, Pard."

"Oh…right…That's why my chest hurts so…I'm really thirsty."

The rancher handed over his canteen again.

Bone took it, removed the cap and held it to Loraine's lips. "Easy, Pard, you don't want to choke. Just take a little at a time."

She took a short drink, a breath, and then another drink. "Thank you."

"Thank the rancher across the way." He nodded across the narrow floorboard between the facing seats. "We managed to get most of the bleeding stopped."

"We?"

"Uh, the lady here and me…She sacrificed part of her petticoat." He mouthed 'and Lucy'.

"Oh…Oh! Loraine said. "I'm really tired."

"Lost a lot of blood, Pard. Why don't you lay your head back down and try to sleep. We got about five hours till we get to Jacksboro."

"Can I sit up?"

"This coach is a little rough. Better stay in my lap, so I can keep you from jostling about…Don't need to start bleeding again."

There was a rumble of thunder from outside.

Loraine nodded and closed her eyes, and then opened them back up. "Did you talk to me while I was out?"

"Uh…Not so you'd notice."

"I swear I heard you call…"

"You need to rest, Pard."

She studied Bone's face for a moment and then closed her eyes. "All right…I…" Loraine drifted off as another roll of thunder pealed across the sky from the gathering dark clouds to the northwest.

WISE COUNTY
ALVORD, TEXAS

Mason and Lucy trotted their mounts along the tree shrouded road just outside of Alvord.

"You feeling stronger, now, Lucy?"

"Yes, thank you. That was an odd sensation…the remote energy transfer through Bone, but apparently effective. He, however, supplied most of the energy…I just helped him to focus."

Mason looked off to the northwest. "Looks like there's some thunder storms brewing. We'll have to put our slickers on if it hits us before we get to Alvord...May make it though. Looks to be 'bout a hundred miles off yet.

That's one thing I don't care for on your planet...Your storms."

"You don't have storms on Tyrin?" asked Mason.

"We have learned how to control the weather...to make it less severe, while still getting the needed moisture for our crops."

"What do ya'll grow?"

"Oh, much the same as here on Tellus, grains, vegetables, fruits...Some of them are different than yours though."

"I guess you feed a lot of the grain to your live stock...cattle, sheep and so on."

"No, we no longer slaughter animals or hunt them for food."

"Really? What do you do for protein."

"We...uh...grow it in a vat. It has the same texture and nutrition as meat here." Lucy ducked her head and blushed. "But, I can assure you...it doesn't have the flavor of your beef, bacon or fish...or any of your game."

There was a long rolling rumble of thunder from the rapidly approaching storm front.

"Probably a good thing you brought your winter coat, too. That cloud bank looks like a cold front...Let's pick up the pace a little," said Mason.

JACK COUNTY

Charlie and Pearly dug out their slickers from under the seat and put them on.

"Better git the neck scarves, too, Pearly. I'm a thinkin' that front gonna be a droppin' the temperature a mite."

"Say, you'd be right, Charlie." Pearly reached back under the seat and pulled out two black heavy woolen scarves.

They wrapped them around their necks and sucked their hats down just as the first downdraft of cold air hit them.

Pearly slid the small sliding window behind him open so he could talk to the passengers. "Better bundle up, folks an' pull down the windows...We're fixin' to git a bit chilly an' wet...I'm a thinkin'."

Loraine blinked her eyes as she woke up from her slumber. "What is it?"

"Gonna have a storm, Pard. Good thing I had Pearly put our saddlebags and coats inside. Looks like we're going to need them."

A loud clap of thunder sounded from directly overhead as the rain started falling in huge drops creating little craters in the dusty road.

The six horses pulling the stage, lowered their heads a little to keep the rain drops from hitting them directly in their eyes.

Inside, Bone lifted Loraine up slightly to drape her sheepskin coat over her.

"Thank you, Bone," she said as she passed out again.

"Want me to hold her while you put your coat on, Deputy?" the rancher across the aisle asked.

He shook his head. "I'll be all right, thanks. She's resting and I don't want to move her."

"You must really love her," commented the woman next to him.

Bone glanced over at her for a moment before he answered, "She's my partner...and my best friend."

"Best ingredients for love that I know of, Deputy…I think she's your *acushla*," she responded with a smile.

"What's an *acushla*? he asked.

"It's an Irish word that means…'pulse of my heart'," said Lollie with a knowing grin.

Bone looked back down at Loraine's face, peaceful in sleep, but still showing some pain, pursed his lips and wrinkled his brow in thought…

§§§

CHAPTER FOURTEEN

ALVORD, TEXAS

Mason and Lucy hunkered down in their saddles as the storm hit just as they arrived at Alvord, in Wise County. They pulled rein in front of Barton's Livery and Wagon Yard on the main street and dismounted as large drops of rain began to patter down. The sun had settled below the horizon.

The tin roof of the stable and porch over the entry of the livery rattled with a machine gun-like staccato from the first wave of rain.

The owner of the livery, Muley Barton, a heavyset man in striped blue bib overalls, stepped out of the semi-dark interior of the stable.

"How do, folks. Need to stall yer mounts do ye?"

"We would appreciate it, Mister Barton, if you have the room," replied Mason. "I'm sheriff of Jack County, Mason Flynn."

"Why shore, Sheriff…an' it jest Muley…Make room if'n I didn't fer your grulla and the child's mule…Fine lookin' animals they are, too." He spat a long stream of viscous tobacco juice in the dry dirt under the roof in front of the entrance. "'Pears as though ya'll got here jest in time…'fore the bottom fell out."

"I'd say," replied Mason.

"Stayin' overnight are ye?"

"We are. Where's a good place to get a room?"

Muley pointed on down the street to a red brick building. "The Alvord Arms Hotel, right down yonder. Clean rooms an' a restaurant downstairs…Good food, it is, too…There's a cheaper place to eat 'cross the street...Bluebonnet Cafe. Cookin' ain't quiet as shiny, though...Know what I mean?"

"I do...and thanks. What do we owe you?"

"Aw, you bein' law an' all, reckon two dollars each fer a stall, hay, grain...an' I'll check their shoes for you an' brush 'em down...Put yer Winchester'n saddles in the office so's I kin lock 'em up."

"Much obliged." Flynn reached in a vest pocket, pulled a folded pad of paper money out and counted off four United States silver dollar notes. "There you go, Muley. We'll be leavin' a little before sunup...soon's it's light enough to see."

"They'll be ready...Enjoy yer stay."

"Thanks."

Mason grabbed their bags from the saddles, took Lucy's hand and they ran across the street to the covered boardwalk that extended the entirety of the block down to the hotel at the corner. They splashed through the gathering puddles and jumped over the multiple piles of horse apples that were scattered up and down the dirt street from the days traffic.

They ducked under the porch over the boardwalk, stopped and both glanced back at the street that was rapidly becoming a river of mud.

"Wonder what he would have charged if you weren't a lawman?" mused Lucy.

"Probably a dollar."

She giggled. "I think you're right."

The rain was coming down so hard it was difficult to see across to the other side as the main part of the cloud bank was directly above the town. The roar of the pounding rain on the porch over their heads made it difficult to hear. Lightning flashed and thunder rolled as the storm showed no evidence of slacking.

"We did make it just in time...Didn't we?" said Lucy.

"Ya think?" replied Flynn, with a smile. "Come on, I could eat the sideboards from a manure wagon."

"Ooh, that's gross, Uncle Mason."

JACK COUNTY

The rain still came down in sheets after an hour as the horses slogged their way through the gummy mud. The coach occasionally slid to the side on the slick road into previous ruts now filled with water.

"Hey, how 'bout some cover back here? Tarp...anything," shouted the shackled outlaw.

"You hear anythin' Pearly?" asked the jehu.

"Naw, Charlie...You?"

"Not a thin'...Not a damn thin'," he answered as he cracked his whip above the horses.

Inside, the drummer commented about the storm as the rain pounded the stage. "Looks like we're in for a dandy."

"Well, except for the occasional side to side slide in the mud, it's not quite as rough as before," commented the rancher.

"Thank goodness for small favors," said Bone as he still cradled the sleeping Loraine in his lap, her head against his broad chest.

"Do you mind if I check her temperature, Deputy? I have three children and it's something I always do when they're sick or hurt."

"Yes, Missus...uh, Ma'am, that would be fine."

"I'm Missus Whitaker, but, call me Lollie."

Bone nodded. "Yes, Ma'am."

She reached over to feel Loraine's face, first with her palm, then the back of her fingers and got a frown on her face. "Oh, she feels a little warm to me, Mister Bone. I think she's getting a fever."

"Oh, boy," he said. "That's all she needs." He looked at the woman. "Is there anything we can do, you think?"

She tore some more strips from her petticoats and folded them into pads. "We can bathe her face, neck and arms with cool damp cloths is the only thing I can think of in this coach."

ALVORD, TEXAS

Mason and Lucy had checked in the hotel, entered the restaurant and taken seats at a square table with a red and white checked tablecloth against the far wall. They had taken their coats off and hung them on the back of their chairs. A middle-aged waitress approached with a smile.

"Welcome, folks, just check in?"

Mason nodded. "Yessum. We're sure glad too...considerin' the storm out there."

Lightning crashed nearby. Everyone in the restaurant flinched, including Mason and Lucy.

The waitress glanced at the windows at the front of the building. "I hate lightning," she commented.

"So do I," answered Lucy.

"My name's Sally, it'll be my pleasure to serve ya'll tonight...This evening's special is fried chicken, with creamed sweet corn, smashed taters an' gravy an' hot yeast rolls with fresh butter...Or you can order a steak, pot roast or beef stew...with the same side dishes."

"Lucy, you go first," said Mason.

"It's gotten so chilly out, I think I'll have the beef stew and some hot tea."

Sally nodded. "You got it, honey. And you, sir?"

"You can bring me a steak, medium rare please, with all the trimmings...Oh, an' coffee, if you please."

"By the way, we have buttermilk pie for desert," Sally winked at Lucy.

"Oh, I just love buttermilk pie," she answered.

Mason chuckled. "That makes two of us."

"Be right back with Lucy's stew...Your steak will take about ten minutes, or less." Sally smiled, turned and headed toward the kitchen.

Flynn glanced over at Lucy and saw she suddenly had a troubled expression on her face. "What's the matter?" he asked.

She frowned. "Bone thinks Loraine may have a fever."

"Can't you and he do that healing thing again?" asked Flynn.

Lucy shook her head. "Dealing with an infection or fever is much more difficult." She looked at Mason. "I'm afraid I will have to make direct contact with her…What time do you think we'll get to Jacksboro?"

He thought for a moment. "If we push the boys…we should be there about noon tomorrow, assuming the rain lets up some."

Lucy grimaced and stared out the front windows of the restaurant at the water dripping from the porch over the boardwalk. "I hope and pray to the Holy Entity it's not too late."

JACK COUNTY

"Would you mind seeing if the driver can go a little faster," Bone asked of the rancher.

"I'll try, Deputy." He twisted around and slid the small wooden window open and yelled against the noise of the storm. "Charlie, Deputy Bone wants to know if you can get a mite more speed out of the team."

"Pushin' 'em hard as I can in this mire," he yelled back.

"Thanks, anyway." The rancher slid the window closed. "Did you hear, Deputy?"

Bone nodded.

"We'll just keep wiping her with these wet cloths," Lollie said as she poured a little more water on her rag from the rancher's canteen.

Bone held his out for the same treatment. He put his cheek against Loraine's. "She really feels hot now…Hang in there, Baby, you hang in there. You can't die on me…not now." He wiped her face with his freshly dampened cloth as the coach slid to the side…

§§§

CHAPTER FIFTEEN

JACK COUNTY

...The stage came to a shuddering stop with a loud bang, and then moved a few more feet before finally coming to rest.

Bone jammed his feet against the opposite seat to keep Loraine and him from being dumped in the floor or on top of the rancher and drummer in the sudden stop. Lollie wasn't as fortunate and was tumbled into the floor between the front facing and back facing seats. The jump seat had been removed before the trip began.

"What the..." Bone exclaimed.

Pearly jumped down from the box on top to the ground on the near side and jerked the door open. "You folks awright?"

"What the hell happened?" asked Bone as Lollie got back up and into her seat.

"Hit a big rock when we slid off the road...Busted a front wheel. We're dead in the water."

"Got a spare?" inquired Bone.

"Tied on top at the back, but ain't got no way to lift 'er up...Left the jack at the smithy's to be worked on," Pearly replied.

"Lollie, can you hold Loraine and stay inside?" asked Bone.

"Yes, of course."

Bone lifted the still unconscious Loraine and placed her in Lollie's lap. "Everybody else out," he commanded.

He, the rancher, and the drummer exited the stage. The rain had slackened to a heavy drizzle, but the coach had lurched to the right. Almost half of the spokes on the right front wheel had shattered and the bent steel rim was hanging askew.

The surviving road agent was laying beside the road where he was thrown on the impact—his neck had broken when he hit the ground.

"Throw those bodies off the top, Charlie," Bone said. "Get that spare and your lug wrench."

The driver rolled the three bodies off the top. "Won't do no good, Deputy…like Pearly said, don't have no jack."

"Just do what I said."

Charlie unfastened the spare front wheel, and clambered down, while Pearly broke out the cast iron lug wrench for the single large axle nut.

"Now what?" asked Charlie.

"Just get that wheel off and put the other one on when I pick up the coach." Bone looked at the rancher. "Hold the leaders still."

"You got it," said the rancher.

"You crazy, Deputy? Know how much this dang thang weighs?" asked Pearly.

"Don't care…Do it," Bone said as he positioned his feet in the mud at the edge of the coach just behind the front wheel, squatted down, slipped his hands underneath and arched his back. "Now."

He bellowed like a bull and straightened his legs. The right corner of the stage and running gear lifted off the ground high enough for the front wheel to clear the ground. Bone stood there like an oak tree, looked up at the cloudy sky, closed his eyes and grit his teeth as the drizzle collected and ran down his face.

"My God in Heaven," muttered Charlie as he quickly fitted the wrench over the large square nut holding the wheel on the axle.

It only took his experienced hands a moment to break the nut loose and spin it off where he could jerk the broken wheel off and sling it to the side out of the way.

Pearly had packed the hub with grease on the replacement, and then rolled it over where he and Charlie could lift it to the axle and shove it on. The jehu spun the nut back on and cinched it down with the wrench.

"Got it!" said Charlie.

Bone dropped the coach and collapsed to his hands and knees in the mud. Charlie and Pearly helped him back to his feet.

"You awright, Deputy?" asked Pearly.

"Just get this son of a bitch back on the road...I'll be fine," he said as he staggered back to the door and jerked it open. "Everybody in, let's go...Let's go."

Charlie and Pearly mounted and took their places in the box. The driver unwrapped the reins from around the brake lever on the off side and held the team as the rancher worked his way in the mud from the lead team back to the off side door.

"What about the bodies, Deputy?" asked Charlie.

"Leave 'em. Weigh too much. Let's lighten the load for the horses...I'll send the undertaker back out from Jacksboro to pick 'em up later...Now let's go," Bone said as he stepped back up inside the coach.

"I'll take her now, Lollie."

"Are you sure?" she asked.

"I'm fine," he said as he lifted Loraine from Lollie's lap to his own like she weighed nothing and fell back in the forward facing seat in near exhaustion.

"Come up there boys...H'yah...h'yah," yelled Charlie as he popped his whip above the team's backs.

The six rested horses dug into the mud, pulled the coach back to the center of the road and continued their trip to the south toward Jacksboro. It was now lighter by four bodies—a little over seven hundred pounds.

Inside, Bone held Loraine against his chest, leaned his head against the back of the coach and took several deep breaths.

Lollie noticed a small amount of blood oozing between his fingers from both hands as he continued taking big gulps of air.

Up in the box, Charlie urged the team on with another, "H'yah!" And slapped the ribbons against their backs. He turned to Pearly as the team picked up speed. "Damnation...That Samson feller from the Bible's got nothin' on Deputy Bone."

The messenger grinned and nodded. "I'm here to tell ya." He pulled out his pocket knife, cut a chaw from his plug of Brown's Mule and stuffed it in the side of his mouth. "Hotamightydamn...Ain't never."

ALVORD, TEXAS

Lucy jerked and dropped her fork back onto the small dish on top of her slice of buttermilk pie. "Oh."

"What's the matter?" asked Mason.

"The stage hit a rock and broke down," she answered.

She had a sharp intake of her breath. "My goodness gracious!" Lucy looked over at Flynn. "Bone had everyone get out except for the woman passenger he had to hold Loraine...He picked the side of the coach up while the driver and messenger changed the wheel."

"There's no way," exclaimed Mason. "It would take three, meby four men to pick up the side of a Concord stage...Impossible."

"Well, he did it and now they're back on the road to Jacksboro," said Lucy.

BONE'S LAW

JACK COUNTY

Lollie reached over and felt of Loraine's forehead. "She feels warmer, Deputy. We better bathe her face, neck and arms with cool water again...Her color's not looking very good."

"See how much longer Charlie thinks it will be to Jacksboro, will you?" Bone asked the rancher.

He twisted around again and slid the small window open. "When do you think we'll get to Jacksboro, Charlie?"

"'Bout another two hours, Herm," he replied.

"You hear him, Deputy?"

"Yeah...Hand me my rag, please, Lollie."

She took Bone's cloth from the seat on the other side of her and poured some water from Herm's canteen on it.

"Oh, by the way, name's Herm Lewis. Run a spread east of Jacksboro...right near Wizard Wells...Cattle and horses."

"Thanks for your help, Herm," commented Bone as he nodded at the weathered face that resembled the Academy Award winning actor, Ben Johnson, across from him.

"Here, Deputy Bone," Lollie said as she handed him the wet rag and then gently wiped Loraine's sweating face with hers.

He bathed her hands and up her arms under her buckskin sleeves.

Bone looked back up at Lewis. "You say Wizard Wells?"

"Yeah, got a couple sections over there, good water an' plenty of graze."

Bone wiped Loraine's hands again. "Don't suppose you know a Corine Waverly?"

"I do. Neighbors...If you call two miles away bein' neighbors...Widow lady...Real loner."

"What does she live on?" asked Bone.

"Well, that's the thing. Rumor has it she had four sons...all outlaws...Two were killed by a posse and the other two were hung by District Judge Miles, over in Cooke County...Folks say her boys left her a bunch of money they had stole from a couple banks 'fore them two were killed an' the other two was hung."

"That a fact?"

"What they say...Said none of the bank money was ever recovered, neither" added Herm. "She's livin' on somethin'."

Bone placed his cheek against Loraine's and looked over at Lollie. "She doesn't feel any hotter...but no cooler either."

"If we can keep it from going up any more, it will be a good sign...You taking her into see Doc Mosier?" said Lollie.

Bone nodded. "Only one I know in Jacksboro. Worked on me a little while back."

"There's a new doctor...a young man that has recently moved to Jacksboro from down south at Cisco. But, I suspect he's still a little green," she replied. "A Doctor Cianci."

"I trust Doctor Mosier," said Bone.

"I understand he was a field doctor in the War of Northern Aggression," Lottie added.

"He should have plenty of experience with gunshots wounds, then," replied Bone. "I was in some action...uh...overseas and our field medics were top notch...Dealing with bullet wounds is a learned procedure."

"My daddy said if a man got shot in a arm or leg in the war, why they'd just go ahead and cut it off...Most died anyway," commented Herm.

"I understand Jacksboro used to be a real wild and woolly town...before Mason Flynn was elected sheriff," commented Lollie. "We've only lived there for almost five years.'

"Really tamed it down, did he?" asked Bone.

"Oh, yes…Of course there is still the occasional riffraff that comes into town, but, he puts the kibosh on them in short order…He's had to shoot a few pestiferous individuals that resisted when he hunted them down."

Bone nodded. "Yes, Ma'am…Worked with him for the last month."

"He's got a reputation for being tough," added Herm. He glanced at Bone's gun on his hip. "Say, that's a real unusual firearm you have there, Deputy…Don't think I've ever seen anything like it."

"It's an…uh…an experimental handgun from Smith and Wesson."

"Looks big…What's the caliber? Sounded like a durn cannon when you shot at those highway men."

"Uh…It's a .50 cal."

"Good Lord…No wonder…It sounded almost like a LeMat my daddy carried in the war…When he fired the secondary twenty gauge barrel…be about the same as a .62 caliber slug…I suppose," said Lewis.

"What's that one Loraine is carrying?" asked Lollie.

"Uh...its a .45 caliber semiautomatic," answered Bone. "Uh...It's also an experimental."

"When she shot those two brigands, it sounded like one shot," said Herm.

"Yeah, she's a good law officer and a heck of a shot," added Bone.

"Like Sheriff Flynn's wife?"

"Yes, Ma'am...A lot like Marshal Flynn," answered Bone.

"I hope she's as tough as Fiona," said Lollie.

Bone looked at her and then back down at Loraine. "Yes, Ma'am...So do I." He took a breath. "So do I." He wiped the sweat from her face.

§§§

CHAPTER SIXTEEN

JACK COUNTY

It was almost ten p.m. when the stage rolled into town with the horses covering the last two miles at a hand gallop. Charlie pulled rein at Mom Tucker's Livery and Wagon Yard, which also served as the stage way station.

"Whoa there boys." He pulled back on the reins.

Mom strode out of the stable, snapping the left shoulder strap to her ever-present blue bib overalls, closed. She was followed by her lanky, strawhaired teenage son, Haircut, rubbing the sleep from his eyes.

"'Bout time, Charlie. What in hell you been doin' to these horses? They're all lathered up an' blowin' like freight trains...You tryin' to wind break 'em? You know better."

"Had to hurry, Mom, Deputy Loraine's been shot. Gotta git her to Doc Mosier's."

"Oh, Lord in Heaven...Haircut, see to the deputy's horses tied to the back, I'll take care of the team."

Bone stepped out of the coach with Loraine in his arms and headed in the direction of Doctor Mosier's office in a long stride. Lollie, Herm Lewis and the drummer followed exiting the stage.

"Bone, is she..."

"Got a fever, Mom," he said over his shoulder.

"Need any help? It's two blocks," she yelled after him.

"No!"

"The only time he put her down in the last five hours was when he picked up the coach so we could change a front wheel we busted," said Charlie.

"When he did what?" Mom asked incredulously, spinning back to the driver.

"He picked up the stage…by his self," repeated Charlie.

"It was a sight to behold, I'm here to say," said Herm.

"One man can't pick up a stage," Mom said.

"Swear on my sweet mama's grave an' poke my eyes out with a stick, he done it…We didn't have no jack," said Pearly.

Mom watched Bone's broad back disappear in the dark down the street heading to Doctor Mosier's office and clinic and shook her head. "Only Bone," she muttered.

Lollie picked up the hem of her travel dress to keep it from dragging in the mud so she could run. She quickly caught up with them and ran on ahead to wake Doctor Mosier.

Lollie pounded on the door and pulled the rope the doctor had installed outside that rang a bell up in his residence on the second floor.

A lamp light appeared upstairs and soon afterward, another inside his office. He opened the door, pulling the suspenders from his trousers over the white nightshirt he still had on.

"What is it, Lollie?" Then he noticed Bone striding up behind her carrying an unconscious Loraine in his arms. "Oh, Lord...Inside, Bone, what happened?"

"Loraine's been shot, Doc a little over five hours ago. Lost a lot of blood...Now she's burning up."

"Damnation...Back here."

He led the way through a door into the clinic area. "Lay her on my exam table there. Lollie, you mind helping me? Gertrude's at home outside of town."

"Of course, Doc. We've been keeping her bathed down trying to keep her temperature under control, but it's been getting progressively higher."

"Need to get this buckskin top off, hate to cut it, but, I see it already has two holes in it and soaked in blood...Can't be saved anyway."

"We can get another made, don't worry about it," said Bone.

Mosier turned to him. "You need to get out of here, Bone, you take up too much room."

"I'll stand in the corner over there, Doc…I'm not leaving her."

The doctor stared at him a short moment and finally nodded. "Probably a good thing now that I think on it. I may need to ask you some questions…plus you can help me turn her over."

"Whatever you want, Doc."

"Fill that pan over there on that table with fresh water from the bucket, and then stoke up the fire in the stove. Going to need a bunch of hot water…quickly. Plus it's getting cold in here."

"Yessir." Bone filled the pan with the dipper, and then opened the stove firebox and added some fresh kindling, stoked the coals up to start it burning, and then added some chunks of split oak firewood on top of the kindling.

Doctor Mosier unbuckled Loraine's gunbelt and with Lollie's help, pulled it out from under her. He handed it in Bone's direction without looking.

Bone took it, pulled Loraine's .45 from the holster and made sure it was on safe. He popped the magazine from the grip, racked the slide, caught the round in the air and slipped it back in the magazine.

He noticed the three rounds missing, removed three from the loops in her belt, reloaded the eight round mag, returned it back to her Kimber and set it with the heel of his hand. Then he rolled the belt around the gun and holster and laid them on the counter behind him.

The doctor took a pair of surgical scissors and cut right down the center of Loraine's top, between her breasts, and then out each arm. He and Lollie eased the top out from under her to get it off.

Loraine was left wearing only her skin-toned jog bra from the 21st century underneath.

"That's an unusual undergarment," said Lollie. "The full figured women I know have to wear whale bone supported corsets or camisoles down to their waists...Wonder where I can get some like this for my millinery store?" mused Lollie.

"Yes, it is unusual, but with the size of her breasts, she needs something like that. Must have had it custom made."

Mosier frowned and muttered, "She's lost a great deal of blood all right...Lollie, take one of those towels, wet it in that basin Bone filled and bathe her down and get that blood removed. You'll have to take that undergarment off...it's soaked with blood, also."

Lollie looked the bra over and then felt under her back.

"There are small hook and eye thingies in the front, there, under that flap," said Bone, pointing.

Lollie glanced at Bone, and then lifted the flap between her breasts, unhooked the fasteners and pulled the bra out from underneath Loraine. "It's elastic."

"Uh...Yessum...Uh, keeps her, ...uh...breasts from jig...uh, bouncing," stammered Bone.

"How did you know where the hooks were?" asked Lollie.

"Uh...My mother was a large breasted woman, too," he nervously replied.

Doctor Mosier removed the blood-soaked cloth pad from Lollie's petticoat that was over the entrance wound and started to examine it. "Already got a good clot, but I'm going to have to remove it and see if I can find out what's caused the infection...My guess is that the bullet carried a piece of her buckskin top into the wound...Cause an infection every time. See how inflamed the tissue is around it?"

Lollie nodded.

"She was shot with a .45, Doc," said Bone.

"Figured." He stepped over to a drawer, opened a small cardboard box, extracted a pair of thin black rubber gloves and pulled them on."

"What are those, Doctor Mosier?" asked Lollie.

"Disposable rubber gloves. The chief surgeon at Johns Hopkins Medical College, a Doctor Halsted, had Goodyear to start making these back in '94 for sanitary purposes. It's almost impossible to get your hands and nails totally clean. These gloves solve that problem...Here, you put these on." He handed her a pair.

"They're too big," she said.

"Doesn't matter...Now hand me those sterilized forceps from inside that metal tray over there on the counter. They're kind of like long skinny pliers."

Lollie removed the lid from the tray and held up a pair. "These?"

"That's right, now take some of that iodine in the jar there on the counter and a cotton pad and clean the area near the entry. We'll deal with the exit wound later."

She wiped the rest of the dried blood from the right side of Loraine's chest and especially all around the entrance hole, staining her skin an orange-yellow. "How's that?"

"That's fine...You'd make a good nurse, Lollie."

"I've got four children, as you know, Curtis."

"Yep, that answers that...Hold that lamp, with the reflector on the back, down close to her chest...That's good."

Mosier leaned over and lifted the edge of the clot loose, and then eased it from the hole. "Interesting."

"What's that, Doc?" asked Bone.

"Not bleeding. I would have expected it to commence again when I removed the clot."

"Well...uh...it has been five hours," said Bone.

"Uh, huh...Maybe. Hand me two probes, Lollie. Look sort of like knitting needles."

She grinned. "That I know about."

Hold the light closer. He used both probes to spread open the wound. That action released a small pocket of pus. "Wipe that please," he said.

Lollie wiped the yellow ooze away with a pad in her other hand.

"Thank you." Mosier pushed the muscle fibers aside and held them. "Ah, hah." He laid one of the probes down, picked the forceps back up and lifted a small bit of a blood-soaked fibrous material from over an inch down inside the wound.

He held it up to the light. "Like I figured. A piece of buckskin was carried into the muscle tissue." He dropped the tiny particle in a small metal bowl and the forceps on the tray. "Hold the light close again."

Lollie did as she was told while Mosier poked around once more.

"Well, don't find any more…so, I hope I got it all." He picked up a bottle of a dilute solution of carbolic acid and poured some directly into the wound to wash it out and disinfect it. "Lollie, wipe it down good again while I get my needle and thread."

After stitching the entrance wound, he and Bone carefully rolled Loraine over so he could inspect the exit hole.

"Umm…Good clot also, but it still needs stitches."

Doctor Mosier went through the same clot removal and cleansing procedure as on the front, and then stitched the quarter-sized exit wound closed with four black linen stitches. There were little puckers in the skin at the top and bottom of the stitches.

"Give that another good wiping down, Lollie."

He watched as she cleaned the area thoroughly, and then nodded at Bone and they turned her back over.

"Move her over to that bed and we'll cover her with a blanket."

Bone picked Loraine up and carried her across the room into the hospital area and laid her onto a small bed.

Lollie opened a glass front cabinet and took a blue woolen blanket out and draped it over Loraine up to her neck.

"Did that get it, Doc? I mean the infection?"

Mosier grimaced. "Time will tell, Bone, time will tell. Hard to know how advanced it was. It was very unusual that there was already a lot of healing…Loraine must have an excellent constitution."

"Oh, she does, I can attest to that."

"Well we'll know more in the morning. I'm just really glad she remained unconscious while I was digging around in there."

He looked at Bone. "You'd better go on over to the hotel and get some rest. We've done all we can do tonight."

"I'll just stay here…if you don't mind, Doc, and keep an eye on her in case she wakes up."

"Well, your choice…If she does, call me, I'll be upstairs." He felt Loraine's forehead and then got a six inch mercury thermometer from the cabinet, put it under her tongue and checked his gold pocket watch. "This takes about five minutes."

At the prescribed time, he removed the glass tube and held it close to the lamp to read the calibrations in it. "Hmm…104 degrees. Hope it doesn't go any higher…but we'll see in the morning.

He undid his stethoscope from around his neck and listened to her heart and lungs. "Don't hear any abnormal lung sounds, so I think they're all right…I'll be down about sunrise."

Mosier turned to Lollie. "Thanks a lot, I really appreciate your help. Now you better scoot on home before Hank comes looking for you."

"Oh, I suspect he's fast asleep, Doctor Mosier." She turned to Bone. "I'll be by tomorrow to check on her too…Gotten kind of attached to her. I can understand ya'lls connection…I'll take her undergarment home and wash it for her before the blood sets…Good night, gentlemen."

Lollie closed the door of the clinic behind her and left out the front door in the office.

Mosier turned to Bone. "What connection was she talking about?"

"Oh, uh…Why, we're partners, is all."

He looked at Bone over the top of his wire-rimmed glassed. "Uh-huh…Say, I never asked, what's your first name?"

"My full given name is Darrell Ulysses Bone, but even my mama just called me, 'Bone'."

Mosier smiled, nodded, turned and headed up the stairs to his residence.

Loraine moaned in her sleep. Bone pulled a chair over and set down beside her bed. He reached over and picked up her hand, held it in both of his and just watched her face as she slept.

Bone looked up. "Please…please, help me," he whispered, and then closed his eyes in concentration. In a moment a stronger blue glow than before began to emanate around their hands.

ALVORD ARMS HOTEL

Lucy's eyes snapped open for a moment in her bed, and then closed again as her lips pursed.

§§§

CHAPTER SEVENTEEN

WISE COUNTY

The sun had just cleared the horizon and the crimson arrows it had cast in the clear morning skies before rising were fast disappearing.

Mason and Lucy held Sailor and Spot at a road trot, headed southwest toward Jacksboro.

Flynn glanced over at the child-size alien. "What are you smiling at, Lucy?"

She looked back at the broad-shouldered, mustachioed county sheriff. "Oh, just that Loraine is doing much better. We're not in such a rush, now."

"What happened?"

"Apparently Bone learned how to enhance his healing power in short order. There's more to your great grandson than you know. He has an extremely powerful spirit," Lucy commented. "It's amazing what you Tellurians can do when you're motivated."

Mason shook his head. "Must have taken after his great grandmother."

"Don't be so modest...It took the two of you to create him through your daughter, his grandmother. You and Fiona were meant to be together...I feel it's written on the Holy Obelisk as was me being here and Bone and Loraine being sent back in time."

"It's all way over my head...How's he going to handle that sniper?"

"He does have an unusual idea, but I'll let him bring it out."

"Aw, come on," chided Mason. "What is it?"

She glanced at him with a half-grin.

JACKSBORO, TEXAS

"I'm hungry and thirsty," said a voice in Bone's ear.

He jerked awake from his slumber in the straight-backed wooden chair next to Loraine's bed.

"What? What?" Bone glanced over to see her propped up on one elbow, looking at him. "I said I was hungry...starving, actually, and thirsty."

Bone jumped up and felt the side of her face.

"What are you doing?" She pushed his hand away with her free one.

"Checking your temperature."

"Why?"

"Pard, if you'll remember, you got shot, and then you developed a fever about five hours out of Jacksboro and passed out. You were still unconscious when we got here...You're in Doc Mosier's clinic."

"Get out of town," Loraine exclaimed and looked around at the room in the dim light. She saw a glass of water on the small table next to her bed, picked it up and drained it.

"If I'm lying, I'm dying...You nearly bled to death, Pard...and then got that infection. Doc went inside the wound and removed a piece of your buckskin top and sewed you up."

"More." She handed him the glass, and then looked down at the bandage on her chest and saw her bare breasts. "Oh, my God! I'm naked," she screamed and jerked the blanket back up to just under her chin.

"Uh...Just half." He grinned. "Your buckskin top was soaked in blood...and...you're...uh, bra was too."

"You saw me naked!" she exclaimed.

"No, no, nothing like that..."

"Damn you, Bone, you did too. You sat there all the time I was talking to you and didn't tell me."

"Well, yeah...but, I didn't look," he quickly responded.

"Bull!...I know you. You'd peek through the key hole if you thought you could cop a look...and where's my bra?" She looked around the room again.

"Uh…Missus Whitaker took it home to wash it for you," he said as he got up filled her glass and set it back down on the table.

"Who's Missus Whitaker?" Loraine asked as she grabbed the full glass and emptied it also.

"Lollie."

"Damn you, Bone…who's Lollie Whitaker?" she said as she set the glass back down.

"Oh, she was on the stage…Helped to keep your fever down by tearing up her petticoats and soaking them in water so we could bathe your face, neck and arms…Plus she assisted Doc Mosier when he fished around in your wound, and then sewed you up."

"What the devil's going on down here," said the doctor as he stepped down from the stairs. "You're awake?"

"Well, of course…It's morning," she responded.

Mosier moved over to the counter in the examining area and retrieved his thermometer.

He shook the instrument down and said, "Open."

Loraine threw a questioning look at Bone.

"Better do it, Pard or he'll find some other place to put it."

She opened her mouth and he stuck it under her tongue. "How do you feel?"

Loraine tried to answer, but it came out muffled and garbled.

"Just nod or shake your head for yes or no...Don't bite my thermometer, it's filled with mercury," he instructed. "Plus they're hard to get."

She nodded and grunted her all right.

"Do you feel weak?"

She did the same again.

He turned to Bone. "Go down to Ruth Ann's and get her a bowl of bone broth."

Loraine groaned, rolled her eyes, and shook her head.

"You lost a great deal of blood, little lady, you need some rich bone broth to start with to help replace the fluids and nutrients...Understand?"

She slowly nodded and frowned with her eyes.

"Damn, I like this...Loraine Rodriguez, when she can't talk," quipped Bone. "Oorah!"

Her dark brown eyes snapped in anger and seemed to almost glow for a moment as she glared at him. There was no question what she was thinking.

"I better go get that broth. Uh…Need a cup of coffee, Doc? I'm getting one."

"Thought you'd never ask, Bone…Gertrude won't be here for another hour to make it. Just bring a whole pot." He glanced back at Loraine. "And yes, you can have some."

Loraine nodded and her eyes smiled as Bone beat a hasty exit after grabbing his coat.

Mosier watched him leave the room, and then stepped over and added some more wood to the heater stove. "There's a chill in here."

Out on the boardwalk, Bone turned to the right to head down to the restaurant, took two steps, spun about and headed the opposite direction.

He strode straight to the Sheriff's office and jail just a half block away.

Bone pushed open the thick wood paneled door with a small barred window at eye level and stepped inside.

Gomer shot to his feet from behind the desk. "Bone, you're back!"

"You're getting real observant, there, Deputy Pyle…Hope for you yet."

"It's Platt, Bone."

"Oh, right…knew that."

Newton pranced over from his spot beside the stove, wiggling all over.

Bone leaned over and scruffed his head. "Hey, boy, miss me?"

Newton woofed and spun around three times and stood on his hind legs for Bone to rub both his ears. "I'm glad to see you, too."

"Where's Loraine?" asked Gomer.

"She got shot…"

"What? Shot? Is she…"

"She's over at Doc Mosier's. He had to stitch up the in and out holes," commented Bone. "Gonna be all right. She's tough as a steak from a two thousand pound bull that died of old age."

"Wow, have to tell me all about it…Oh! You got a telegram yesterday afternoon." He picked up the yellow envelope from the top of the desk. "From Marshal Lindsey up to Ardmore."

Bone took the telegram, opened it and extracted the flimsy. "Thanks, Gomer, and by the way, you need to go out to Lisanne's and get her and Slim…We turned seven horses loose up about 20 miles north on the Henrietta road where those highway men tried to hold up the stage…Need to pick up the four bodies we left on the side of the road, too…Tell Lisanne she can have the horses."

Platt's eyes got big. "Yessir, I can do that."

Bone looked down at the telegram. "Hmm…Missed seeing the Johnson boy, going back today. Seems he was out hunting…Uh, huh." Bone muttered, "Hunting what?"

He turned and headed out the door. "Got to go get Loraine some hot broth and me and the doc some coffee."

"Know about the broth thing. Been there."

"Emma Lou's bringin' some breakfast from Sewel's for our guest in the back in a bit, then we'll come over."

Bone stopped and looked back at the deputy. "What'd he do?"

"Oh, got drunk an' rowdy down to the Coolwater last night and shot a couple holes in the ceilin'. Didn't hit nobody upstairs…Had to whack 'im upside the head with my gun barrel, though."

Bone grinned and nodded. "You're learning, Gomer. Sometimes there's only one way to deal with a belligerent drunk."

"Yessir, findin' that out," he said to the door as it closed.

It didn't take long for Bone to get down to Sewell's after stopping at the hotel and getting Loraine her olive drab T and BDUs she was wearing when they were transported back to 1898 through the Indian portal. He had stuffed them in the large patch pockets on the sides of his sheepskin jacket.

Emma Lou brought him out a bowl of steaming broth on a wooden tray with a napkin and soup spoon.

"Oh, me and the doc could use a pot of coffee, too, if you don't mind," said Bone.

"Of course, I'll bring it by on my way down to the jail to take a prisoner his breakfast. I'll be right behind you."

"What do guests of the county get for breakfast these days?"

"Gomer said he'd probably be a mite hung over, so I fixed him up some grits an' butter. My sweetheart said he'd get some coffee down him." She giggled. "And I know how he makes it."

"Yeah, me too…Grits. The staff of life."

"We'll stop by Doctor Mosier's and visit Loraine on the way back."

"I'm sure she'd appreciate that. Gomer already told me...Laterbye," Bone said as he headed to the door.

Mosier removed the thermometer and read it. "98 point 7...Close enough...Amazing." He slipped the instrument in upper front coat pocket of his white hip length coat he wore in the clinic.

"Well, let's take a look at your wounds." He leaned over and pulled her blanket down far enough to get to the bandage on her chest.

"It feels pretty good, Doc, honest," Loraine commented.

"We'll see," he said as he peeled the adhesive tape loose from the gauze pad over the stitched hole.

Lollie Whitaker came through the door from the front. "Well, I didn't expect you to be awake."

Loraine looked over at the matronly, attractive brown-haired woman, with a puzzled expression.

"I can tell you don't know who I am. I'm Lollie Whitaker..."

"Oh, you were on the stage and helped Bone with me, and then helped Doctor Mosier stitch me up last night."

"Yes, that would be me...You look so much better than you did yesterday. You've gotten your color back...We were really worried about you, expecially Bone." She handed Loraine a package. "I also removed your undergarment and took it home with me...Wanted to wash it before the blood set."

"My undergarment?"

"To support your breasts," said Lollie.

"Oh, my bra," said Loraine as she undid the brown paper wrapping. "Oh, thank you. That was so nice."

"Your what?" asked Lollie.

"Brazier...It lifts and supports. We just call it a bra in my...uh...where I come from."

"This can't be," Mosier said as he carefully lifted the pad away, fearful of it sticking.

"What? What's the matter?" asked a startled Loraine as she tried to look down at where she had been shot.

He looked up at her, and then back down. "Nothing...It's healed. There's no way...but it is. I can even remove the stitches...Sit up and lean forward so I can see the exit wound."

Loraine held the blanket to her chest, sat up and twisted a bit so he could get to the dressing on her back.

Lollie stepped closer so she could see.

"I don't know what to think...or say. It's healed also. I don't mean just closed, but the skin has knitted back together and formed some red scar tissue...overnight. Impossible."

"What's that, Doc?" asked Bone as he came through the door with the tray.

"There's been a medical miracle, here, Bone." He palpated the larger back wound. "That hurt?" he asked Loraine.

"Not really...I mean it's a little tender, but no pain like yesterday...The times I was awake, it burned like it had a hot knife poking in it," she added.

"I don't understand it," said Mosier as he leaned back and shook his head. "I thought I'd seen a lot of things, but, this is something else all together...I would write it up, but none of my colleagues would believe me...Not sure I believe it myself."

Lollie turned to Bone. "What about that thing you were doing yesterday in the coach before we left that made that thin blue glow? You said something about learning it from a Shaman. Could that have caused the healing? It certainly helped the bleeding."

"Uh…"

§§§

CHAPTER EIGHTEEN

JACK COUNTY

Lucy giggled as she and Sheriff Flynn trotted along the still slightly muddy road to Jacksboro, about twenty-five miles away.

Mason glanced over at her riding Fiona's paint mule, Spot. "What now?"

She shook her head and giggled again. "Bone's being asked by Doctor Mosier and the lady from the stage who saw him the first time when he tried the healing procedure on Loraine, if the blue glow had anything to do with her healing." Lucy giggled once more.

"Uh, oh," commented Mason.

"It's going to be interesting to see how he dances around the answer."

JACKSBORO

"Uh, I have no clue, Lollie, I didn't see anything…Maybe it was just some dust lingering inside the coach from when we rode up."

"No, no, not dust. It was blue and soon afterward, her bleeding stopped. You mentioned something about giving her some of your spirit or soul because she was dying and you learned it from a Shaman," said Lollie wagging her finger at him.

Mosier glanced at Bone with a puzzled expression on his face.

Loraine realized what had happened from when Lucy worked on Bone when he was shot and jumped in, "I've always clotted up real fast, plus healing quickly...Never understood it, but I do."

"There's no belying results. But, I've never seen healing that fast in my forty years of practicing medicine," said Doctor Mosier. "Who was that..."

Bone jumped interrupted, "Oh, say...Uh, here's that broth, Pard. Better eat it while it's still hot." He carried the tray over to Loraine and set it on the table. "And here's your T and BDUs. I imagine you want to put something on and change those buckskin trou, they got blood on them too...We can see if Sing Lu's Laundry can get it out."

She glanced up at him from the top of her eyes. "You think?...How about you turn your big butt around so I can do that?"

"Oh!...Right...I'll just step out into the waiting room," he said, pointing, as he quickly went back through the door and closed it.

"You do that," said Loraine just before the door closed. She looked back over at Lollie, and then at Doctor Mosier. "He's just like a big kid, sometimes."

"Maybe, but I heard him pray to God for help to save you." Lollie grinned. "He loves you, you know," she said, more as a statement than a question.

Loraine slipped on her bra, snapped it, and then pulled her T over her head. "Bone?" She chuckled. "Not likely...We're just partners...Cat and dog partners, but partners, nonetheless. Bone doesn't love anyone, but himself."

"I mean more than partner love...He's *in* love with you," replied Lollie.

"That's...that's ridiculous," Loraine stammered.

"I think you're going to find out differently...sooner or later and I'm betting on sooner," Lollie said with a big grin.

Loraine smiled and shook her head. "I could see myself with a lot of people...but, Bone? Not in this time line...uh, I mean lifetime." She got up from the bed, pulled off her buckskin pants and slipped on her BDU trousers. She weaved a little and quickly sat back down.

Lollie smiled back and crossed her arms over her bosom. "Uh, huh...I saw him mothering and praying over you...I watched him caress your face while the tears ran down his...and talking to you while you were unconscious."

"Bone?"

"Yes, Bone." Lollie cocked her head and studied Loraine for a long moment. "You're not kidding anyone, you know, my dear...unless it's yourself. You're both running from it, but, it's there and you can run, but you can't hide from it...forever. It's going to hit you one day and hit you hard...Wait and see...and remember that Lollie said so."

"There's one thing I know, and that is we men will never understand the opposite sex...and I don't think we were ever meant to," commented Doctor Mosier. "The noted Austrian psychologist, Sigmund Freud, is considered by his peers to be the most knowledge man in the world about women, based on his papers...He was reported to have said privately, 'Women...Dear God, what do they want?'"

"Of course, Curtis. Now I know why you've never married," commented Lollie, smiling.

"I have had my share of dalliances, madam...but I prefer to maintain my sanity."

"I think that's why God made us this way." She looked at Doctor Mosier and then at Loraine with a twinkle in her eye. "Keeps things interesting, you know."

BONE'S LAW

Bone opened the door a crack and stuck his head in. "You decent? All done?...Keeps what interesting?"

JACK COUNTY

"Well, that was masterful."

"What?" asked Flynn.

"The way Bone and Loraine teamed up to deflect the questions about her healing and redirect them to another subject."

"Really?...They do make a good team," Flynn said.

Lucy grinned and nodded. "Uncle Mason, you may one day have a great grand daughter in law...Loraine," said Lucy with a smile.

He laughed. "Is that it?" he chuckled again. "Fiona told me that not long after Bone took that bullet from old man Sinclair, meant for her, when she and Bone went after him and his boys after they captured Lisanne and Steeldust."

"I know," commented Lucy, with an impish smile.

JACKSBORO

It was almost noon when Mason and Lucy reined up in front of Mom Tucker's Livery and Wagon Yard.

Mom's teenage son was collecting fresh horse manure from several piles, over by the water trough, with a grain scoop and dumping it in a wooden wheelbarrow.

"Haircut...Mom around?" asked Mason as he stepped down, walked around Sailor's rear to Spot and helped Lucy to the ground.

"Yessir, Sheriff...She's in the office takin' care of some paperwork. I'll fetch 'er for you." He leaned the short handle of the big wide shovel against the wheelbarrow and trotted inside.

In a moment he came back out with Mom in tow. "Well, didn't expect you back just yet, Sheriff. Where's Fiona and the buggy?"

"Still at my sisters. Lucy and I came to see about Loraine...She at the Doc's?"

"Last I heard," Mom replied as Mason and Lucy turned and started walking toward Mosier's office.

Mom headed back inside, but stopped, looked over her shoulder at them already on the boardwalk.

"Huh? Now, wonder how they knew?" She took her corncob pipe from the pocket in the front of her bib overalls and packed it from a leather pouch.

Mason and Lucy approached the front door of Doctor Mosier's clinic. He reached out to grasp the knob.

Down two blocks at the end of the street and on the opposite side—a rifle barrel glinted in the sun. A figure in a dark broadcloth suit and dark gray slouch hat crouched on the roof of the single story Jack County Cattleman and Merchant's Bank, behind the parapet. The dark clad figure rested the '76 Winchester on top of the short brick wall and sighted in on Sheriff Flynn's chest.

"Mason!" Lucy screamed and shoved him hard against the side of the red brick building just as the boom of a rifle sounded.

Flynn's limp form slumped down the wall to the boardwalk as Lucy covered his body with hers.

211

The door sprung open and Bone ran out, almost tripping on Mason's body. He glanced down at Lucy on top of him and looked up the street to see a cloud of gunsmoke over the roof of the bank building two blocks down and across the street, slowly drifting off in the soft breeze.

He sprinted toward the building as Doctor Mosier stepped out of his office and knelt down beside the sheriff. Lucy got to her feet and watched Bone charging in the direction of the bank.

He quickly reached the red brick building and ran around the back to see a set of wooden stairs leading to the roof. Bone took the steps, three at a time to the top with his 500 drawn. "Damn...nobody." He turned to the east to see a bay horse and its rider galloping away, already almost a quarter of a mile distant. "Shit," he muttered.

He walked over to the front and glanced around, spying a brass shell next to the parapet. Bone picked up the still warm casing with a pencil from his parfleche hanging at his side. "Uh-huh...A

.50-95 caliber…Probably a '76 Winchester like Teddy Roosevelt's."

Bone looked to the east again at the rider just topping a hill over a mile in the distance. He turned around, headed down the stairs and jogged back to the clinic.

He reached the office and saw Mason's body already gone from the boardwalk. Bone ground his teeth together, grabbed the doorknob and pushed the door open into the clinic.

Mosier's regular receptionist and nurse, Gertrude, had arrived at work just before he walked in. She was setting her purse on the desk and turned around at Bone's entry. "Oh, Mister Bone…"

"The doc and them inside the clinic?" he asked.

"Yes, I'm sure. Just got here so I really don't…"

"Thanks," he opened the door to the clinic and stepped inside.

Doctor Mosier, Lollie, Lucy and Loraine were gathered alongside the examining table where Mason's body lay.

Loraine looked around with a frown on her face.

Bone walked toward the table. "Is he…"

§§§

CHAPTER NINETEEN

ARBUCKLE MOUNTAINS
ELK, CHICKASAW NATION

Marshals Jack McGann and Selden Lindsey reined up outside the old Dalton cabin, now occupied by their cousin, Thelma Johnson and her son.

"Horse ain't much punkin'," said Jack noticing a swaybacked, spavined bay gelding in the corral.

"Must be twenty or twenty-five years old," added Selden.

"Helloo, the house," yelled Jack.

In a moment, the wafer thin Thelma Johnson came out of the door and stood on the rickety front porch. Her arms were folded in front of her almost nonexistent bosom. She was wearing the same worn gray cotton day dress and a stained white apron she had on two days earlier.

"See you lawdogs is back. Reckon you be wantin' to talk to my boy."

"Yessum, you don't mind," said Selden.

"Wouldn't matter if'n I did, now would it?"

"No ma'am, 'spect not," replied Jack. "Just tryin' to be polite."

"He be 'round back, a dressin' out a deer he kilt." She turned and went back in the house.

Jack and Selden exchanged glances, turned their mounts and walked them around back, between the cabin and barn.

"Her demeanor ain't changed much," said Selden.

"Noticed," replied Jack.

Jessie James Johnson was underneath a large red oak, skinning a gutted buck, hanging upside down from a thick limb. He had over two-thirds of the hide cut loose and pulled down to the deer's front legs. The young man whose straw hair looked as if it had been trimmed with a hunting knife. He was still in the process of cutting the skin away from the fascia.

His rifle was leaning against the trunk of the tree. Jack and Selden both glanced at the weapon before they dismounted.

Jack leaned over to Selden and whispered. Sharps Carbine…'64…converted, I'd say."

Selden nodded and said sotto voce, "Uh-huh Confederate duplication…brass fittings, not iron. Looks 'bout wore out."

"I'd say…Nice buck, Jessie," said Jack as he and Selden walked up.

"Thankee, thankee kindly," the scruffy young man replied.

"Was beginnin' to think I wadn't gonna get one an' ma would be powerful upset, till I seen this 'un a grazin' on acorns under a burr oak this mornin' 'bout sunrise."

"This is US Deputy Marshal Jack McGann an' I'm US Deputy Marshal Selden Lindsey."

"How do, Marshals. Ma said ya'll wuz by an' wuz comin' back."

"How'd you git him home?" asked Selden.

"Ol' Buck carried 'im. He's my horse over yonder in the corral. 'Bout wore him out...he's a tad older'n me, but he done good."

Jack picked up the Sharps from against the tree and looked it over. "Shot 'im with this, did you?"

"Yessir...All I got. Beats throwin' rocks at 'em. I reckon...It's a mite worn. Gotta git fair close...Only got two cartridges...Now I got one."

Jack handed it to Selden.

"Kindly loose, ain't it?" said Lindsey.

There was a thin strip of rawhide the boy had wrapped around the stock foregrip to hold it to the barrel.

"Yessir, purty beat up."

"Where'd you git this 'un? asked Jack glancing at the carcass.

"South of Hennipin some. Five, six miles I reckon."

"That's north of here, ain't it?" asked Selden.

"Yessir. Foothills of the Arbuckles…Further than I wanted to go, but we need the meat."

Jack and Selden looked at each other and nodded.

"Understand…Say, I'm wonderin' if you can do me a favor," asked Jack.

"Shore, Marshal…if'n I kin."

"I got a box of .50-75 cartridges I taken off a ne'er-do-well we arrested. Don't fit any of our weapons an' they're jest weightin' down my saddlebags."

Jack stepped over to Chief, his Overo paint gelding, and pulled the box from his saddlebags. "Reckon you kin take 'em off'n my hands? Know they don't fit yer rifle there, but meby you kin take 'em in to Elk next time you go and trade 'em in fer some that fit your Sharps…Save me a bunch of trouble."

Jessie scuffed the ground with his worn brogans and then looked up at Jack. "Well, ma don't cotton much to taking charity an' such."

Jack grinned. "Ain't charity, boy, I was fixin' to chunk 'em. Tired of totin' 'em around…Be doin' me a big favor." He handed the box out to Jessie.

The young man looked down at the box like it was candy, paused a moment, and then took it. "Reckon I kin...It bein' a favor an' all."

He glanced back up at Jack and then to Selden. "Marshals, I been a kindly a wonderin' what a feller would have to do to become a law...like ya'll?"

Jack and Selden exchanged glances again. Selden stepped over to his black stallion, Dan, got a .44 Remington and a box of shells out of his saddlebags and handed them to Jessie.

"Tell you what do, son. You practice with this some.

"That the gun you took off'n Mad Charlie last month, Selden?" asked Jack.

"One in the same." He looked back to Jessie. "Now you git comfortable with it and we'll come back in a month er two and see how yer doin'...When you git where you kin handle it real good...Well, me an' Jack will recommend you fer a deputy job with Town Marshal Waycock over to Elk...He purty much takes whatever we say as gospel...What say?"

"Oh, wow!" Jessie exclaimed, his eyes tearing up. "Ya'll'd do that fer me?"

"Why, shore. You look like a fine, upstandin' young man to me...You, Jack?" said Selden.

"I'd say, Selden. Git the impression the boy wants to make somethin' of himself."

"Yessir! I do. Been thinkin' on becomin' a law fer a long time...'Specially with what my daddy done." He looked down at the ground. "He was really a good man at heart, Marshals...He jest didn't know what else to do to feed me an' mama...Tol' me he didn't go to kill that feller, but he pulled a little lady pistol on 'im and Pa got all nettled an'..." He turned and leaned his head against the tree, his body racked with sobs.

Jack stepped over and put his arm around the young man's shoulder. "Think we understand, son, but, what's done is done...No need in wallowin' in it. I like the way yer thinkin'."

Jessie turned around, nodded and wiped his eyes with a worn blue bandana. "I won't let you down, Marshals...God as my witness, I won't." He straightened up and pulled his shoulders back and nodded at Jack and Selden.

"Don't think you will, either, Jessie. Don't think you will," said Selden. "Now, I'd suggest you git on about dressin' that fine buck 'fore the blow flies find it."

Selden and Jack stepped over to their horses.

"Yessirs…an' thank you again."

"We'll see you in a month 'er so," said Jack as he swung into Chief's saddle.

He and Selden turned their horses and trotted off back toward the old dirt road leading up to the cabin. Without looking back, each waved good bye to Jessie James Johnson.

When they were on the trail that headed toward the road back to Turner Falls and Jack's home, Marshal McGann turned to Marshal Lindsey.

"Don't know when I felt better about anythin' than helpin' that boy head down the straight and narrow."

"Yeah, me neither…Hey, who the hell is Mad Charlie?" asked Selden.

Jack grinned. "Damn if I know, just goin' along with your story…Knowed that was yer back-up pistol."

"Can git one off the next miscreant I gotta arrest…They break the law, lose their weapons.

'Nuff said…Didn't that box of .50-75s go to yer Marlin?"

"Did."

"Figured."

"Come back in a month er six weeks, see how he's doin'. Bring him some decent clothes, boots an' a Stetson. Cain't go in to see Town Marshal Waycock 'bout a job lookin' like a urchin or ragamuffin," said Jack.

"You remember his mama don't take to charity."

"Remember…I'll take my little note takin' book have him sign for the duds on account…Jest won't never call the bill," said Jack.

"On account?"

"Yeah…On account I want to." Jack had a big grin on his mustachioed face.

Selden nodded and joined him as they trotted on down the trail toward home.

JACKSBORO, TEXAS

Mason sat up on the examining table as the others turned to look at Bone coming in the door.

"No, I ain't, Bone. Lucy saw the sun glint from the rifle just before the sniper pulled the trigger and shoved me into the wall. Banged my head on the brick corner of the door frame…Reckon it rang my bell."

"Actually I felt the evilnesss which prompted me to look around and up along the roof tops. That's when I saw the rifle."

"Can't believe you could shove me into the wall like that. You're not big as a nickle," said Flynn, still holding a damp pad against the egg-sized knot on his head.

Lucy smiled and winked. "I'm stronger than I look."

"Ya think?" replied Mason.

"Look at me," said Doctor Mosier.

Mosier studied Flynn's eyes a moment as he passed a pencil back and forth in front of them. "Well, if you're concussed, it's a very mild one."

"Fiona always says how hardheaded I am."

"I don't think that's what she was referring to, Mason," said Loraine.

"Speaking of…how are you, Miss Rodriguez?" asked Mason.

"Other than being weak as a kitten, I think I'm all right."

"I believe I know what happened," commented Doctor Mosier.

"Oh," questioned Lollie. "Would you care to elucidate?"

"I think Bone used what the ancient Chinese call *Reiki*...or energy healing. It's somewhat analogous to the 'laying on of hands' as in the *Tanakh* of the ancient Israelites. There is reference to it in *Leviticus,* also. Plus there are many references to Jesus using the laying on of hands in the New Testament."

"You mean I'm like Jesus?" inquired Bone.

"Not in this lifetime, Bone, you just figured out a way to tap into your energy to make me feel better and speed up the healing," said Loraine with a wry smile. "Probably more like some ancient Chinese priest." She turned to Doctor Mosier. "Didn't they eunuch them?"

"Well, whatever," Bone replied.

"Did you spot anything when you ran off to where the shooter was?" asked Lucy.

Bone shook his head. "Just this." He took the pencil from his parfleche again and lifted the spent casing out. "Found this on the roof of the bank. .50-95, most likely from a '76 Winchester…saw the sniper riding off to the west…Gonna see if I can pull a print from this brass."

"Won't do any good unless we match it with the shooter…when we catch him," said Loraine.

"And we're going to catch him, Pard," replied Bone.

The door opened and Gomer and Emma Lou came in. The deputy handed Bone a note.

Bone put the pencil and the spent casing back in his parfleche and closed the flap.

"Got a call on that new telemachine we got in the office from Marshal Lindsey," said Gomer.

Bone opened the note and read it. "Just says we can take Thelma's boy off the list. His and Jack's opinion is that it's impossible the boy could be the shooter. Explain more later…Selden."

"Well, guess that puts Cobb on top of the list. Still need to go talk to the widow Waverly, so we can take her off," said Loraine.

"To quote Sherlock Holmes, 'when you have eliminated the impossible, whatever remains, however *improbable*, must be the truth'," added Bone.

"'Elementary, my dear Watson...The game is afoot'," said Loraine with a grin.

§§§

CHAPTER TWENTY

SHERIFF'S OFFICE

"Lucy mentioned you might have a unusual idea, Bone?" Flynn said.

Loraine, Lucy, Bone, Flynn, Gomer, and Emma Lou, each got a cup of coffee from the pot from

Sewell's Restaurant. They all found a place to sit in the crowded office.

Lucy sat cross-legged on the floor next to the glowing potbellied stove, beside Newton, scratched behind his ears and nodded. "I think Bone would be the best to explain it."

Bone coughed and cleared his throat. "Well, that's the thing. You see, I was thinking we could rig up a way to make it look like Mason was killed and that would make the last of the posse dead and gone."

"But, Bone, he was just almost killed a little bit ago," said Loraine.

"Right, now you're getting it, Pard. We don't have to set anything up."

"Oh! Of course. We put out the word that Sheriff Mason Flynn has been murdered and the funeral will be in a couple of days at the Jacksboro Memorial Cemetery," commented Loraine.

"He was knocked out and assisted inside Doctor Mosier's office before any towns people arrived," she continued.

"Considering how fast Bone was out the door, there's no way the shooter could tell if they hit

Mason or not, with him lying on the boardwalk," said Lucy.

"They apparently ran immediately after firing the shot. The gunsmoke cloud in front of their rifle would preclude them seeing their hit," said Bone.

"But, how does that help find the sniper?" asked Mason.

Bone grinned from ear to ear. "I guarantee you that when the shooter finds out that you…the last of the posse, died of their gunshot wound today, they'll get sloppy and over confident because they'll think they've accomplished what they set out to do…We'll make sure the paper carries a story about County Sheriff Mason Flynn being assassinated."

"They completed their retribution mission and might even brag about it," added Loraine, nodding. "Good, Bone, real good…Can't believe I'm saying that."

"How do we make it work?" asked Flynn.

"Well, one, you have to play dead. We'll even have a funeral as soon as Fiona can get here," said Bone.

"But, how do we tell my Fiona that it's all just a ploy?" asked Flynn.

Bone and Loraine exchanged glances.

"We can't," said Loraine.

Mason shook his head. "Oh, boy..." He got up from behind his desk and paced around.

"At least till she, your sister and Cletus get here...Certainly can't put it in the telegram," interrupted Bone.

"Yeah, right, I get it...But, I'm still goin' to catch mortal hell from both Fiona and Mary Lou when they get here for puttin' them through this, you know?" said Mason.

"They can jump on me," commented Bone.

"We have to let Doctor Mosier, Lollie and Gertrude in on it, because they saw you unhurt except for the lump on your head," commented Loraine. "They'll have to swear to secrecy."

"That's why you put Bone's hat an' humongous coat on me when we came over here from the doc's office," said Flynn.

"Yup," replied Bone. "You'll even have to hide out back there in a cell." He pointed to the cell area. "Till Fiona and them get here...Then, since I'm sure they'll be coming in Cletus' buckboard, we'll pull it around behind the jail, slip you in the back and cover you with a tarp till ya'll get out to your ranch." He turned to Gomer. "Deputy, would you mind going over to the Western Union office and send a telegram?"

"Sure, Mis...uh, Bone. Just write out what you want it to say."

Bone sat down behind the Sheriff's desk and wrote the text of the telegram on the notepad. He tore the page off, folded it and handed it to Gomer.

"Here you go, slick. Gotta send it to Cletus Wilson at Rosston.... Don't need to wait on an answer, they'll have to take it to Cletus and Mary Lou, at their ranch."

"Then ya'll can go out to Lisanne's and tell her and Slim about those horses we turned loose...Need to tell the undertaker, too. He'll have to take his big buckboard for the four bodies," said Bone.

"Yessir. Come on, Honey," he said to Emma Lou.

They grabbed their coats and headed out the door.

"Loraine and I will go on out to Wizard Wells and talk to the widow Waverly in the meantime...You up to it, Pard?" asked Bone.

"Yeah, after I eat half of everything on Sewell's menu…I'm starving. That broth didn't go very far," answered Loraine.

"Better watch it though. Those BDU trou don't have stretch waists…or seats, you know."

"Damn you, Bone, don't judge everyone by yourself," said Loraine.

He chuckled. "Come on, let's go on down…You coming, Lucy?"

"Yes, I'm hungry also."

"We'll bring you something back Mason," said Bone. "They don't have to know Gomer already turned that sobered up drunk out after he had his grits this morning."

"How 'bout a big bowl of Ruth Ann's son of a gun stew on a cold day like this?" asked Flynn.

"Oh, that sounds good," said Loraine as she grabbed her coat.

Bone, Loraine and Lucy opened the door to Sewell's Restaurant, ringing the two inch brass bell attached to the header. They had already stopped at the doctor's office to fill him and Gertrude in on the plan, and then at Lollie's Millenary to clue her.

Ruth Ann's sister, Molly met them at the door. "Ya'll come on in. Do you want the Sheriff's table? I'm assumin' he's comin' in a few minutes?"

"Uh...Well, Molly, uh, Mason won't be coming...He was shot and killed just a bit ago by a bushwhacker right in front of Doctor Mosier's office. The doc couldn't help him...He's...he's gone, Molly...He's gone," Bone's voice broke a little as he finished speaking.

Loraine and Lucy both dabbed their eyes with hankies.

"Oh, no...No! Not Mason. Please, no...Dear God. It can't be." Molly instantly staggered back a step and began to tear up.

Loraine put her arm around Molly's shoulder. "We know, Molly, we know. We're all stunned."

"Does Fiona know?"

"No, not yet. She's still at his sisters. We had to send a telegram. They're on their way," said Loraine.

"Oh, Lordy, Lordy." Molly shook her head.

"We thought we better get something to eat before it got too busy...You know, notifying everyone and all," said Bone. "We're going to have ya'll son of a gun stew, and need to take a bowl back to the jail for our guest."

Molly wiped her eyes again. "Ya'll go ahead and take your seats over yonder." She pointed toward Flynn's regular table against the wall. "I'll bring it right out. What are ya'll having to drink?"

Bone looked at Loraine, she nodded. "Coffee for me and my Pard...Lucy?"

She thought for a moment. "Think I'll have hot chocolate."

Molly forced a smile. "All right, Honey. Be right back." She turned and headed toward the kitchen.

They walked over and took their seats at the table.

"How're you feeling, Pard?" asked Bone.

"Still weak as a kitten, but I'll be all right."

"There's not much the healing procedure can do about blood loss. You'll have to let your body replace that on it's own...It takes a little time," said Lucy softly after looking around to make sure no one could hear.

Loraine nodded.

"You know, Pard, think you ought to stay here this afternoon with Lucy and Mason and rest while I ride over to the widow's...Somebody needs to stay at the jail with our guest since Gomer is going to have to go up north with Lisanne and Slim anyway."

Loraine contemplated her condition and replied, "Well, I suppose so. Just that walk down here from the office almost did me in."

"Thought as much, Pard."

"Don't want to push it, Loraine," said Lucy after glancing at Bone.

Loraine nodded her agreement.

"Here you go, folks," said a still teary-eyed Molly as she set three bowls of stew on the table along with a basket of hot yeast rolls and a saucer of fresh butter from her tray. "Be right back with your coffee and hot chocolate."

"Tell you what you can do while I'm gone, Pard," said Bone.

"Uh-oh, here we go," Loraine answered. "Do I need to grab my ankles?"

"No, really, come on, Pard...go down to the Jacksboro Gazette and give them the full story. We'll contact the Baptist church about holding the services there...You can take that casing I picked up on the roof of the bank and see if you can pull a print...I'll leave our kit."

"Oh, piece of cake. Just like home...What if I have to arrest somebody?"

"Just do what we do a lot back home...Give them a warning, put the fear of God in them and tell them to be on their way."

Loraine nodded and smiled. "Yep, used to that."

"I imagine that trip out to Wizard Wells will be a water haul, but it has to be done...Eliminate all possible persons of interest."

"That's the way it's done, Bone," said Loraine with a grin.

"As you said, Pard, just like home...gotta do the footwork."

After lunch, Bone walked down to Mom's Livery to get Hildebrandt.

"I heard," said Mom as he walked up. "Just a damn shame...A cryin' shame. He was such a fine man."

"That he was, Mom. He taught me a lot," commented Bone as he snugged Hildebrandt's cinch after Haircut walked him out of the stable.

"Won't be gone long. Gotta go out to Wizard Wells...What is it, about six or seven miles?"

"'Bout that…You watch yourself, that assassin might target you next," warned Mom.

An hour after Bone left Jacksboro, following the directions from Mason, he rode under the entry of the Circle W Ranch.

§§§

CHAPTER TWENTY-ONE

CIRCLE W RANCH
JACK COUNTY

"Pretty well kept place…Bet it costs a buck or three to keep it up. What do you think, son?" Bone mused to Hildebrandt as he trotted toward the large, rambling, green shuttered, white shiplap, ranch style house with a three-sided wrap-around porch and three red brick chimneys. The galvanized standing-seam tin roof looked new.

Hildebrandt didn't reply. "Yeah, me too," said Bone.

He glanced to his right at a large board and batt red barn with a white plank corral adjoining. There were two bay geldings inside, working on a couple of flakes of alfalfa on the ground.

"Hmm, that's interesting."

He reined up at the fence around the front yard. There were well-kept flower beds all along the front of the porch and out the flagstone walkway to the gate. An elderly woman sat in a tall wicker-back wheelchair on the porch, sipping on a small glass of some type of light amber liquor.

"How do you do, Ma'am. Are you Missus Waverly?"

"I am, who are you and what do you want?"

"Deputy Sheriff Bone, Jack County, Ma'am, like to have a word with you."

"Step down, then, big man. Tie up that giant horse you're riding and come on up."

"Thank you, Ma'am," said Bone as he tied Hildebrandt to the hitching rail, loosened his girth, went through the gate and up to the porch.

He noticed the elderly woman's face was seamed like the bark of an old oak tree, her long snow-white hair was in a single thick braid behind her head, but her eyes were still a bright blue. She wore an expensive looking dark blue linsey-woolsey dress with a white lace wide collar, buttoned up to her neck and had a matching wool shawl around her shoulders against the chill.

"Would you like a shot of a 12 year old, double malt scotch or are you here on official business?"

"Official business, Ma'am, but thanks for the offer...Mind if I sit?"

"Might as well, not fond of lookin' up to folks...especially not one as tall as you...nor officers of the law."

Bone sat down gently in a slat-back rocker near her wheelchair.

"How can I be of service?" she asked.

"Missus Waverly..."

"Call me Bertie."

Bone nodded and continued, "Uh...Bertie, do you leave the ranch much?"

"Only when I need to, why? As you can see, my perambulations are quite limited...I can't get around by myself. My housekeeper, Marie, takes care of me."

Bone looked around admiringly. "Oh, I can certainly see why you wouldn't leave much anyway, nice place...Just wondering if you'd been to town recently?"

"Like I said, only when I have to. Don't care for towns much."

"I take it you don't go in for supplies, and such...Just to get out."

"No, I send the hired help in for that. I have no need or desire to *get out*...as you say."

Bone looked around and glanced back at her, starting at her ankle high buttoned shoes with a small heel, and then up to her peeress, patrician face. "You mentioned hired help, where are your hands, by the way?"

"Out checking on the stock, can't get much done hanging around the house."

"You run cattle here, do you?"

"Cattle and horses. I'm working on developing a new breed of cattle. One with the thriftyness of longhorns and the beef of a whiteface, but better milkers and more resistant to insects and the heat, like longhorns."

"Mixing in some shorthorns?"

"I see you know something about cattle."

"Some, yes, Ma'am. Enough to know a breeding program is too expensive for my blood."

"It can get that way, yes, but if you're wondering, I have an inheritance and I brought in some bulls of a new breed from India called Brahmin. They are considered holy over there...They don't eat them...Named after the Hindu priests."

"Yes, Ma'am, heard of them. There's some folks in south Texas crossing them on various breeds for the same traits you mentioned."

"It's the coming thing...Now, I'm sure you didn't come out here to talk cattle, Deputy..."

"No, Ma'am...We lost our sheriff, Mason Flynn, this morning...He was murdered..."

There was no change in her expression as she replied, "Pity."

"He was the last of a posse that tracked down murderers and thieves back eight or nine years ago...They've all been murdered...bushwhacked in the last month or so. You know anything about that?"

"Why should I?"

Bone's gold flecked amber eyes locked on her blue ones. "Your four sons were tracked down by that posse. Two were killed resisting arrest..."

"They were shot down like dogs, by paid assassins," she hissed with gritted teeth.

"...and the other two were hung for their crimes."

"By an evil, flannel mouth, narcissistic judge."

Her eyes turned to an almost slate color, like storm clouds, and became hard as steel. "I think I've enjoyed about all of your company I care to, Deputy. Don't let the gate hit you in the back on your way out...Good day." Her gaze never wavered from his, nor did she blink.

Bone's face showed his enigmatic smile as he rose to his feet. "Yes, Ma'am, you have a nice day...Hear?" He touched the brim of his dark green John Bull hat, and then went down the five steps to the walkway.

He stopped and turned around. "The sheriff's funeral will be in a couple of days. We're going to have the service at the Baptist church...if you're interested."

"I'm not," she said, almost smiling and downed the rest of her drink.

"As you wish."

Bone continued on out to his horse. He snugged up the cinch and swung easily into the saddle and headed back toward the front entry, squeezing Hildebrandt up into a road trot. He shrugged both shoulders as if to loosen the tightness he felt in the center of his back.

"Not a happy camper, there...is she, Hildebrant?"

Bone reined up in front of the Western Union office next door to the stage depot across from Sewell's Restaurant when he got back to Jacksboro and went inside. In a short moment, he came back out, mounted and rode on down to Mom's and stepped down from his saddle again.

She strode out from inside and took the reins to Hildebrandt. "Git yer errand done?"

Bone nodded. "I did." He turned and headed to the sheriff's office.

BONE'S LAW

ARBUCKLE MOUNTAINS, IT
MCGANN CABIN

Marshal Selden Lindsey pulled rein outside the white picket fence around the front yard of Jack and Angie McGann's large log home. "Hello, the house," he yelled.

Angie stepped through the white gingerbread screen door followed by Son, their white wolf/dog, Baby Sarah and Aurali Red. The two children waved at the familiar Marshal.

"And what are ye doin' at me house, Selden Lindsey? It's not dinner time," said Angie.

The marshal stepped down and wrapped Dan's reins around the hitching rail outside the fence. He opened the spring-loaded gate and walked toward the porch.

Jack came through the door behind Angie and the kids. "Uh-oh. I know that look. What's happened, Sel?"

He pulled a telegram from his inside coat pocket and held it up.

"You know me too well, Jack. Guess they ain't no easy way to say this, but...Mason Flynn's been murdered..."

"Saints preserve us!" said Angie as she brought her hand to her mouth.

"Who done it?" asked Jack.

"The sniper got him in Jacksboro right in front of Doc Mosier's office."

"Anybody see 'im?"

"Apparently not, the telegram doesn't say. Just said the funeral is day after tomorrow. We kin catch the afternoon train, if we get a move on."

"I'll be throwing some things in a bag, Selden, you and Jack go harness up the buckboard. I'll get the children ready, too...Have ye told me uncle *Anompoli Lawa*? I know he was quite fond of Mason."

"Yep, told him just before I came out. He'll meet us at the train an' Bodie'll pick us up at the station in Gainesville."

Angie shook her head. "My sweet Jesus, such a wonderful man he was...I'll be needin' to get to Fiona. I know what's she's goin' through and her bein' pregnant and all." She turned and ushered the children back in the house.

BONE'S LAW

SKEANS BOARDING HOUSE
GAINESVILLE, TEXAS

Bodie Hickman, his wife Annabel and their twins, Bass Lee and Cassie Ann and the proprietor, Faye Skeans, sat around the parlor with a crackling fire in the fireplace. Bodie was having coffee and his wife and Faye, tea. The twins, just toddlers, were playing with their toys in the floor. There was a knock at the door.

Faye got up, walked through the foyer and opened the ornate front door with the etched and frosted glass in the center. The red brick Queen Ann style three story house had been built in 1878 by Faye's cattle baron father.

"How do, Miz Skeans...telegrams for Ranger Hickman," said the gangly, dark-haired teenager as he removed his short-billed, flattop Western Union cap.

"Come in, young man. He's in the parlor," said Faye as she turned and led the way.

The young man walked straight over to the large, rawboned, redheaded Texas Ranger and held out the yellow envelope. "Telegrams for you, Ranger, want me to wait for answers?"

"Well, let's see, bub," said Bodie as he opened and removed the flimsies, and then read first one, and then the other. "Oh, damn," he muttered, pursed his lips and looked back up at the messenger. "Yeah, say this."

The young man took out his note book and stub of a yellow pencil and looked back up.

"Deputy Bone - Sorry to hear about Mason...stop. Protection not needed for Judge Miles...stop. Passed away two weeks ago of stroke...Annabel and me, Doctor Ashalatubbi, Marshals McGann and Lindsey will catch the morning stage...stop. Texas Ranger Bodie Hickman."

"And this to Ardmore...Marshal Lindsey - Will pick you and the McGanns up at station...stop. Texas Ranger Hickman." He pulled out a Morgan silver dollar from his vest pocket and handed it to the messenger. "Keep the change."

"Wow, thank you, Ranger, sir. Get this right out, you betcha." He nodded, tipped his hat at Annabel and Faye... "Ladies." ...turned and headed to the door.

After he closed it behind him, Annabel asked Bodie. "Bad news, wasn't it?"

He took a breath and nodded. "Mason was murdered this morning in Jacksboro...the sniper."

"Oh merciful Heavens," said Faye.

"Oh, no...Poor Fiona, bless her heart." Annabel's eyes filled with tears.

"Jack, Angie, Doctor Ashalatubbi and Selden coming down on the afternoon train. I know it's scheduled to arrive at 6:10 this evening."

"I would love to go to the funeral. I so admired Sheriff Flynn, but the babies don't need to go. I'll mind the twins and the McGann children while ya'll go," said Faye. "Frances Ann may bring her youngster in too."

"That's so sweet of you, Faye," said Annabel with her deep Alabama drawl. "What time is the morning stage, husband?"

"Eight o'clock."

§§§

CHAPTER TWENTY-TWO

JACKSBORO
SHERIFF'S OFFICE

Bone raised his fist to knock on the door since Loraine had locked it when he left to keep anyone from just barging in and seeing Mason.

Before he could contact the wood frame with his knuckles, the door opened.

"Lucy! How did you know it was…Oh, never mind," he said as he looked down at a smiling Lucy.

Bone slipped out of his sheepskin jacket and hung it on one of the pegs in the wall beside the door along with his hat.

"Got any coffee?"

"Does a bear live in the woods?" replied Loraine.

"They do other things there, too, Pard…Guess I have to get it myself."

"Unless your leg is broken…then yes."

"Hey, don't feel bad, had to get mine too, Bone…an' I'm dead," commented Flynn.

"Playing dead," said Loraine.

Lucy was near the potbellied stove. She stood on her tiptoes, reached up, grabbed a white porcelain cup from a shelf on the wall. "I'll get it, Bone…but I'm not going to make it a habit," she said with her pixie face breaking into a grin as she filled his cup and handed it to him.

"Thanks, Lucy. At least somebody loves me."

"You're just a big lovable bear, Bone."

"More like a grizzly," said Loraine.

"You know, they'll name a children's toy bear after Teddy Roosevelt in 1902," said Bone before he blew across the top of his coffee and took a sip.

251

"Why?" asked Flynn.

"Well, he goes on another bear hunt in Mississippi with the governor of the state four years from now in 1902 and he never saw a bear.

"One of his assistants, a former Confederate cavalry man and prewar slave named Holt Collier, trapped a young bear and tied him to a tree. He came and got Teddy to come shoot it…Well, ol' Teddy didn't think that was very sporting, since the bear could neither run, and was too young to defend itself…He refused to shoot it."

"Knowing Mister Roosevelt like we do, it doesn't surprise me that he wouldn't," said Mason.

"That's not the end of the story."

"Are you going to make us beg to hear it or just dangle it out there like a carrot?" asked Loraine.

"Don't get your panties in a wad, Pard, I'm getting there…Now, you see, this cartoonist, named Berryman, publishes a political cartoon of Teddy refusing to shoot the cub.

A candy maker in Brooklyn, New York, one Morris Michtom, whose wife made stuffed toys for children, saw the cartoon and had his wife make a stuffed bear and he dedicated it to President Roosevelt…and called it *Teddy's Bear*.

"In our time, 2018, it's been shortened a bit to just the *Teddy Bear* and after 116 years, is still one of the most popular children's toys in all of the world."

"Is there going to be a quiz, Bone?" asked Loraine.

"No, but that's a thought, Pard...Hey, a better idea is to contact that Michtom fellow in New York and have him make a stuffed Mexican female cop with big hooters...Call it Double D Cop."

"Damn you, Bone," she drew back her arm to throw her cup at him.

"Don't do it, Loraine, that's my last cup. It's a set Fiona got me," said Flynn.

Loraine frowned and set it down. "Your time's coming, you big lug...Just wait."

"Promises, promises...that's all I ever get."

"You'll think 'promises' when I get through with you."

"Now she's getting romantic again," quipped Bone.

"Damn you, Bone...Sometimes you irritate the hell out of me."

Lucy, who had been looking back and forth between the two of them like it was a tennis match, giggled.

Flynn shook his head. "What's the story on the widow Waverly?"

"Well, that's the thing. She looked older'n dirt, not counting the fact she was in a wheelchair...I got real bad vibes just being around her."

"Wheelchair?" said Loraine. "Well, I guess we can take her off the list."

"Ah...Not so fast, Pard."

"What do you mean, Bone?" asked Mason.

"There are some things that don't add up...Haven't got my head wrapped around it as yet. It's like Marcellus' comment to Horatio in Shakespeare's Hamlet...'Something is rotten in the state of Denmark.'"

"Is that the same Horatio that Hamlet spoke to when he picked up the skull and said, 'Alas, poor Yorick! I knew him, Horatio, a fellow of infinite jest, of most excellent fancy.'"

"Dang, Pard, didn't know you read Shakespeare," said Bone.

"Don't. Just heard the quote before."

"Bone's right, Loraine, he makes for good reading," said Lucy. "I acquired his entire works when my mate, Garin and I came to Tellus in the late 1700s."

"How old are you, Lucy?" asked Mason.

"Almost 2,000 of your years."

"You're funnin' me."

"No, you see our life span as a race is actually around four hundred of your years, but since we use what you term, worm holes, which are warps in the fabric of space and time, we can actually reach our destination within moments of departure...It's 107 light years, or 33 parsecs, from my planet of Tyrin to your planet, Tellus..."

"Do what?" questioned Mason.

"You have to understand the space-time continuum and quantum physics," said Bone. "Lucy will explain all this to me and my Godfather, Padrino, in the future when we first meet."

"Come again?"

"It's referred to in our time as the theory of relativity," said Loraine.

"That's correct and considering the number of times we have traveled here through a warp or fold in the fabric of time and space, well, the faster you travel, the slower time goes...and it's not necessarily linear...But I will age normally as long as I'm on your planet. In reality, if there is such a thing, my chronological age is around 200 Tellurian years...as you count it..."

"There's a writer in our time who said, 'They say that none of us exists, except in the imagination of his fellows, other than as an intangible, invisible mentality.' His name is Edgar Rice Burroughs," said Bone.

"Say, I met a soldier, named Edgar Rice Burroughs, with the 7th Cavalry in Arizona when I went out there to get a prisoner in '97 and bring him back here for trial."

"That would be him. He becomes an extremely popular and prolific writer of adventure novels with around eighty books published...They even name a town in California after one of his characters."

"I'm sorry I asked...Ya'll are making my head hurt," commented Flynn.

"Don't feel bad, Mason. Said the same thing back in...or up in, 2014 when I said...or will say it when Lucy explains it," said Bone. "But, like I always say...When you don't know that you don't know...it's a whole lot different than when you know that you don't know...until you know it," commented Bone.

"Huh?" questioned Mason.

"Never mind, I'm just now beginning to understand it after four years or will be four years when she tells me in the future."

Mason shook his head.

"Now, back to the widow Waverly," said Loraine.

Bone took another sip of his coffee. "Not ready to say, yet, Pard. I gotta figure it out first. My gut tells me the old gal's involved some way, but I have to reconcile her age and that wheelchair."

"You know what you always say, Bone," commented Loraine.

"Which one, Pard. I'm like Gibbs on NCIS and his fifty plus rules...that have never been written down."

"The one that goes, 'Always trust your gut'."

"Oh, that's number two," said Bone.

"What's NCIS?" asked Flynn.

"It's a TV show in our time about a crime investigator for an agency of the Navy."

"Your time is way too complicated for me," said Mason.

"I sometimes feel the same way, Sheriff," replied Bone with a chuckle.

"Anyone know what time it is?" asked Mason.

Bone glanced at the dive watch on his wrist. "Almost five."

"Fiona an' them should be gettin' here soon," he replied.

"They're just coming into town, as we speak," said Lucy.

"How do you know, Lucy?" asked Loraine.

"You forget that Fiona is a sender, also. Neither she nor Mason are as strong as Bone, but the combination of their genes is made him that way."

"Just don't forget, smell's not everything, Bone," Loraine shot at him.

The big man grinned and made a motion with the sound effects of an arrow striking him in the heart. "Sssshuup," he said as he thumped his chest with his closed hand. "Good one, Pard."

Lucy got to her feet from her spot on the floor beside Newton and walked to the door. "They're pulling up now, I'll go out and greet them."

Lucy opened the door and stepped out on the boardwalk just as Cletus reined the team to a halt.

"Whoa up there, boys."

Fiona and Mary Lou stepped down, both their eyes were red from crying.

"Oh, Lucy," Fiona said as she hugged the diminutive alien, her body shook with sobs.

Cletus stepped down and tied the matched pair of Standardbreds to the hitching rail with the lead line attached to the off side horse, nearest the boardwalk, and then he stepped up beside the ladies.

Lucy glanced up and down the street. "Fiona, ya'll need to come inside before I can say anything…I think there's someone you want to see." She turned, opened the door and led the three inside.

Fiona and Mary Lou both dried their eyes with their hankies and exchanged confused glances.

Mason had stepped back behind the thick door to the cell area. When Lucy closed the door behind them, he stepped out.

Fiona staggered and put her hand to her mouth, and then rushed forward to embrace her husband. "Mason, Mason, oh, thank God."

"I'm so sorry, Baby. I'm so sorry," he said to her as he held her tight.

Mason's sister also rushed over and embraced both of them.

Finally, Fiona stepped back and wiped her eyes and stomped her foot on the floor. "Mason Flynn, do you know what you did to us?...Why? Why?"

Mary Lou whacked him across his chest. "You nearly killed us, Mason Lee!"

"I'm so sorry..."

"Let me explain it, Mason...Ya'll can jump on me. It was my idea," interrupted Bone.

Fiona, Mary Lou and Cletus all turned to him.

"We're listening...and this better be good or great grandson or no, I might just shoot you," said Fiona.

"I know, I know, but the situation presented itself and seemed like the best course of action, to not only protect Mason, but also to pull the sniper out in the open."

Fifteen minutes later, Bone had completely filled in the story.

Fiona shook her head and embraced Mason again. "I can understand why ya'll did it...but it doesn't make the hell we've been through in the last six hours any easier." She took a deep breath.

Mary Lou joined in, "And if something like this ever comes up again, mister, you better figure out a different way...Do you hear me?"

Mason looked at his feet and said contritely, "Yes, Sis."

"So, what's the next step?" asked Fiona.

"Well, Cletus can pull his buckboard around behind the jail and we'll hide Mason under a tarp in the back and ya'll can go out to the ranch until the funeral services day after tomorrow. We sent telegrams to Bodie, Jack, Doctor Ashalatubbi and Selden and expect them here tomorrow," said Bone.

"Jack may be the one to shoot you," said Fiona.

"Yeah, I know."

"We need to make this look real. Bone and I feel the sniper will show up at either the church services or at the graveside," said Loraine.

"Don't think they'll be able to hold it in when they discover that they somehow missed and that Mason is not dead," added Bone.

"Sort of a modified Trojan horse?" stated Fiona.

"Somewhat," said Bone "Actually, sort of reversed…Mason will be in the casket at the services…Until it's time for him not to be."

"Do what?" asked Flynn.

§§§

CHAPTER TWENTY-THREE

SANTA FE DEPOT
GAINESVILLE, TEXAS

The big black 4x4x2, coal-fired, Gulf and Colorado Railroad locomotive from Denver through Oklahoma City, chugged to a stop just past the red brick platform. The engineer released pressure from the boiler with a loud hiss and huge cloud of steam.

Texas Ranger Bodie Hickman and his willowy, blond wife, Annabel, waited outside the three passenger cars watching for Jack, Selden or Doctor Ashalatubbi to exit one of them. Faye Skeans held the hands of their twins beside them.

"There they are," said Annabel as she waved at Aurali Red holding Baby Sarah's hand when they stepped down the four metal steps to the platform. They were followed by Angie, Jack, Selden and Doctor Ashalatubbi.

"Faith an' it's good to see you, Annabel," Angie said as she hugged the Alabama girl and then Faye. "It's so nice of ye bein' willin' to ride herd on our wee ones, Faye."

Eleven year old Aurali Red immediately bent down and hugged Cassie Ann and then little Bass. "We're going to have so much fun."

The twins hugged her back, and then hugged four year old Baby Sarah.

Bodie shook hands with Doctor Ashalatubbi. "Good to see you, Doc."

"Good to see you too, Bodie." The venerable, white-haired, Shaman hugged Annabel and Faye.

"Oh, I so wish I could go and pay my respects to Fiona, but my place is here." Faye looked down at the children. "Frances Ann Durbin is bringing little Walt, Junior, in so he can play with the others."

"Sheriff Durbin sends his condolences and wishes he could go also, but he's short two deputies," said Faye.

"I'd rather take a whippin' with a wet rope than to go to Jack County under these circumstances," said Bodie. He looked at Jack. "Bass comin'?"

He shook his head. "He's way up in the northern part of the Cherokee Nation the other side of Tulsa on a trackin' down some whisky peddlers."

"Looks like they 'bout got Chief and Dan unloaded...We'll cinch up and meet ya'll over at Faye's," said Marshal Lindsey. "What time's the mornin' stage?"

"Eight o'clock," said Bodie.

"We're gonna ride behind, you gonna ride with us or inside with the ladies an' *Anompoli Lawa*?" Jack asked the ranger.

"Reckon I'll ride Lakota Moon along with you an' Selden. Won't be so crowded inside."

Selden grinned. "Figured...Won't be near as rough, neither."

"All aboard...For Denton, Fort Worth, Waco, Austin, Houston and Galveston...All aboard," yelled the dark blue uniformed conductor as he walked along the platform.

Jack and Selden headed down to the livestock car where the Santa Fe livestock steward and the hostler waited with their horses.

The others followed Faye to her double-seater Phaeton carriage waiting out in the street in front of the depot.

The engineer blew the whistle and the train gave its first chug as the drive wheels first slipped a little, and then started to turn. The cars banged with the start as the train slowly chuffed and gathered speed, headed south, belching black smoke from the stack.

SHERIFF'S OFFICE
JACKSBORO

"Hope Jack and them don't have any problems on the stage from Gainesville," said Mary Lou.

"With two Deputy Federal Marshals and a Texas Ranger along…God help the brigands that try."

"Oh, that's right, Fiona," she replied, almost embarrassed.

"That's definitely a hand to draw to," said Mason, with a smile. "Three men that are tougher than nails."

"Not only that, but, they're the kind of friends that don't come along very often," commented Bone. "That's one of the reasons I wanted them here for your funeral."

"God, that sounds really odd…"

"What's that, Hon?" Fiona asked.

"Talking about your own funeral."

"I've decided I'm not showing up to mine," said Bone.

"Excuse me?"

"Actually, I think he's serious, Fiona," replied Loraine.

"I am," added Bone. "Say, guess we should go down to Ruth Ann's and get some supper."

"Sounds good to me," said Cletus.

"Ya'll need to put on your acting shoes and look in mourning," commented Bone.

"Won't be hard. We've had practice all day, thank you," replied Fiona. "What do you want us to bring you back, dear?"

"You know, believe I'll have one of Bone's pizza pies…Sausage with mushrooms…Big as a wagon wheel," Flynn answered.

"What kind of pie?" asked Mary Lou.

"It's not a desert, Mary Lou…It's a main course meal Bone brought from the future and showed Ruth Ann how to make…Even though they do have them in New York…It's an Italian dish and is absolutely scrumptious…sausage or almost any other type of meat and other toppings, mozzarella cheese, with marinara sauce, on a thin crust," answered Fiona.

"Believe I'm ready for a pizza, too," concurred Bone. "We better boogie, before Ruth Ann runs out of dough."

"Boogie?" asked Cletus.

"A euphemism we use in our time, means to hurry. It's referring to a fast and active dance," said Loraine.

"If we had some four/four time music, we could show you…Couldn't we, Pard?"

"That's another thing we do well together," said Loraine.

"What's the first?" asked Fiona.

"Catch bad guys."

She and Bone bumped fists, opened them to flat palms facing down and pulled them back simultaneously wiggling their fingers.

Lucy grinned, nodded and winked at Fiona.

They all put on their sad faces and headed down the boardwalk to Sewell's Restaurant.

The door tinkled as Bone opened it for the ladies to go first, then he and Cletus followed. Molly met them with her sad face on, too, and led them over to the side wall where she put two tables together for six.

"Be right back with a menu," she said.

"Won't be necessary, Molly, we'll have two large sausage with mushroom pizzas, extra cheese, and we'll need one to go," commented Bone.

She half smiled. "You're in luck, Ruth Ann has a fresh batch of dough for the evening crowd. The aroma from your order is going to make everyone else that comes in want one, too."

"That's a good thing…Nothing smells like a pizza," said Loraine.

After they finished their pizzas and slices of Ruth Ann's special peach/apple pie, Molly brought the take-out one on a platter with a clean dishtowel draped over the top.

"I went ahead and cut it for your prisoner, Bone, knowing you wouldn't allow him to have a knife."

"Good thinking, we appreciate it, Molly," replied Bone. "Oh, could I have another slice of that wonderful pie to take back. May have to have some more," he winked at Molly.

"Like you told me, Bone, our buckskins and BDUs don't have elastic waists," quipped Loraine.

"I work mine off, Pard, plus I can spread it over my six feet eight frame...What are you going to do?"

She stuck out her tongue at him. "I'm not going to eat an extra one, that's what."

"Then suffer while you watch me eat mine." Bone flashed a big grin at her.

Molly brought the slice of pie on a small plate with another towel over it. They pushed their chairs back, got to their feet, headed out the door and back to the office. Bone carried the pizza while Mary Lou carried the pie.

"Good move, Pard, covering me ordering that extra slice of pie for Mason."

"Figured out what you were doing and played along," Loraine replied.

Cletus knocked on the door and waited a moment till Flynn threw the steel bolt back, unlocking it and stepped back out of the opening while the others came in.

"Swear I could smell that pizza when ya'll were still a block away," said Flynn.

"Yeah, so did three dogs roaming the street, followed us all the way here. Too bad, I expect that Newton will get any leavings," commented Bone.

The Border Collie spun around three times, stood up on his back feet and barked twice.

"I see you, Newton," said Mason. "You can have the end of the crust, son."

The dog woofed again.

Bone set the pizza on the desk while Flynn took his chair behind it and lifted off the towel.

"Um, um, um," he said.

Mary Lou set the pie beside it.

"Oh, no, we didn't bring a fork," she said.

"Hey, baby sis, don't need a fork. Bone showed me the proper way to eat a slice of pizza and that..." He lifted the towel from the pie.

"…peach/apple pie ain't gonna be a problem either."

"Heathen," said Mary Lou.

Mason leaned over and sniffed deeply of the still warm confection. "Uh-huh, love me some peach/apple pie, too…Yes I do."

"Dang, you got a point there, Sheriff, may have to jog back down to Sewell's and get me another slice for a night time snack."

Loraine shook her head. "Yep, there you go, Bone."

"Said I'd jog, didn't I?" He flashed his grin.

"What time is the Gainesville stage supposed to get here," asked Fiona.

"Should be here about four or so tomorrow. Leaves Gainesville at eight in the morning," answered Bone.

"I'm goin' to stay here in the jail with Mason, tonight. Ya'll getting rooms at the hotel?" inquired Fiona.

"Think so…rough trip from the ranch…"

Loraine interrupted Cletus. "I've already reserved rooms for ya'll and added the Hickmans, Jack, Selden and Doctor Ashalatubbi for tomorrow night when they get in."

"Good thinking, Pard," said Bone.

"I know."

"Guess you and I should make our rounds and check in on the Coolwater Saloon before we call it a day, Pard."

"Probably. Got our job to do and Gomer and them aren't back from getting the horses and the bodies of those road agents," answered Loraine.

"I expect we can have a Kool-aid or four while we're there," added Bone.

"What's Kool-aid?" asked Fiona.

"Oh, just what we call a drink in the future," answered Loraine.

"Ya'll certainly have confusing times there," said Mary Lou."

"You definitely don't want to hear about my world, then," commented Lucy.

Changing the subject, Mary Lou said, "Going to be a little crowded back in the cell, Mason, guess Fiona will have to sleep in one of the others," said Mary Lou.

Mason glanced over at Fiona and winked. "Oh, I think we'll work something out...don't you, Baby?"

"I would imagine," she said winking back.

"Where there's a will…there's a way," commented Bone with his enigmatic grin.

§§§

CHAPTER TWENTY-FOUR

COOLWATER SALOON

"After you, Pard." Bone opened the right side of the nine-foot tall outer doors, and then pushed open the inner batwings. The solid outer doors were closed on cold days to hold the warmth from the two heater stoves inside.

"Doesn't smell any better than it did the last time we were in here," said Loraine.

"You were expecting lilacs and roses?" replied Bone.

She shrugged. "Guess not."

"Beer?"

"That'll do."

They sauntered over to the bar. The patrons familiar with the pair quickly parted to give them room.

"Couple of beers, Truman," Bone said to the balding, skinny owner/bartender. "What flavors do you have?"

"Budweiser or Lone Star..." He glanced around. "But, I might recommend a new drink I just got...Cactus Wine."

"Oh, and just what is *Cactus Wine*?" asked Loraine.

Truman leaned over and whispered. "Tequila and peyote tea...Ain't got no hellova lot, but it's right tasty."

"Sounds dangerous," said Bone.

"Oh, it don't take no hellova lot. Some of these cowboys just don't know how to drink it."

"If it's good 100 percent blue agave, then it should be sipped and savored neat," said Bone.

"Who makes this Cactus Wine?" asked Loraine.

"It comes from the Sauza family in the Mexican state of Jalisco," commented Truman. "It's a bit pricey, but I think it's worth it."

"Jalisco…That's the only place in the world that produces the extract from the blue agave plant that can be called Tequila," added Bone.

Loraine glanced over at him. "I'm impressed, Bone."

"I'm not just a pretty face, you know, Pard."

"Oh, God help me," she said as she hung her head, and then looked up.

"Like I said, it's pricey…fifty cents a gill as opposed to twenty-five for regular rye or sour mash."

"Wow, is high." Bone winked at Loraine. "Well, I'll give it a try…You, Pard?"

She nodded. "Let's go for it…Oh, what's a gill?"

"Four ounces."

"Works for me," said Bone.

Truman took a bottle from the back bar, set two glasses on the polished St. Louis bar and filled them almost to the top.

Bone laid a Morgan silver dollar down, picked up his glass and held it up to Loraine. "Here's to you, Pard."

She picked hers up and clinked with his. "And here's to a good man, Sheriff Mason Flynn…God rest his soul."

"I thought he was a bastard," said a large rough-looking cowboy down the bar.

"What'd you say, slick?" answered Bone.

"One, my name ain't slick and two, I said he was a bastard…Locked me up in his jail purtnear ever time I come to town."

"Well…slick. Could be you broke the law in some way," said Loraine.

"You best watch yer mouth, girly. Don't tolerate no damn woman smart mouthin' me." He threw back his shot of the house rye.

"Uh-oh," said Bone with a grin. "You just crapped and fell back in it, slick."

"Said my name wadn't slick."

"You're lucky we refer to you any way at all, rather than hauling you down to our steel hotel," said Loraine.

"Haw! I ain't broke no laws, girly," he responded.

"Isn't there a law against being ugly, Bone?" she asked.

"Uh...Don't think so, Pard, but there is one on being stupid...Time and effort will take care of ignorance...but stupid is forever."

The cowboy turned to face Bone and Loraine. "You callin' me stupid?"

"Oh...I'm sorry if I hurt your feelings when I called you stupid...I thought you already knew," said Bone with a grin.

"Huh?"

Bone turned to Loraine. "See?"

"Everyone has the God-given right to be stupid, Bone...on occasion. And numb-nuts here seems to want to make it a habit," added Loraine.

"Awright, that's it, I've had it. Woman or not, Deputy or not, I'm gonna just paddle yer ass."

"You know...*slick*, I see you got two choices," said Bone.

"Yeah, jest what's that, big man?"

"One, we can take you down to the lockup or I can just let you tangle with Deputy Rodriguez here and get completely embarrassed that a woman half your size can whip your ass...What's it going to be?...Your choice."

"Haw, this is goin' to be quick."

He stepped forward.

"Don't you know it's rude not to remove your hat when talking to a lady?" asked Loraine as she did a high sweeping kick that was just a blur. It took his hat from his head and sent it across the room where it landed on a table with four men playing cards.

The room burst into laughter.

The cowboy looked over at his hat, and then felt the top of his head. "How'd you do that?"

"Oh, it was easy," she said as she did the same thing with her other leg, this time catching the side of his nose with her heel, snapping it to the left and breaking the bridge in the process.

Blood spurted from his nostrils as he grabbed it with both hands. "Ow, ow, ow...You bitch, you broke my nose."

Loraine grinned and nodded. "For starters."

"Damn you," he hissed as he lunged forward to grab her.

Loraine snap kicked with her right foot, catching him full in the mouth, popping his head back this time. Several teeth went flying, one landing on the bar and another in the brass spittoon next to the foot rail.

"Better quit while you're ahead...slick. The only way to get out of a hole is to quit digging," said Bone after he took a sip of his Cactus Wine. "Um-good."

"Hell you thsay," he mumbled through rapidly swelling lips and charged at Loraine again.

She stepped to the side, grabbed his arm on the way by and gave it a quick twist, flipping the two hundred pound cowboy in a complete somersault in the air causing him to land flat on his back, looking up at a grinning Bone towering over him at his feet.

His mouth worked several times without anything coming in or out.

"You know, slick, my partner normally has a great tolerance for stupidity...but not with those who are proud of it. You keep this up and she's liable to hurt you." He took another sip.

The cowboy finally got his breath back and looked up at Loraine standing over his head. "You gonna haul me down to the jail now?"

She looked at Bone and then squatted down on her haunches. "How about I let you go with a warning…and the knowledge that I'm going to hurt you really, really bad the next time you disrespect our sheriff…or me. Are we clear?" She thumped his nose with her forefinger.

"Ow…Oh, yesth, Ma'am, you thshore don't have to tell me twicth," he said through his missing front teeth and crushed lips.

"And don't call me Ma'am." Loraine got back to her feet and glanced over at a grinning Truman. "Give this reformed miscreant one of those tequila drinks…on me. When he gets up."

She leaned against the bar, picked up her Cactus Wine and took a sip. "Ooo, that is nice…Smooth as silk."

The rest of the customers in the saloon broke their stunned silence with a roar of laughter and a rousing standing ovation.

"Turn and take a bow, Pard, your fans are calling," said Bone.

She shook her head, turned to the rest of the room, nodded once and then turned back and took another sip. "One more round, Truman." Loraine glanced at Bone. "I got this one."

"Whatever you say, Pard," he replied as he finished his drink.

It was 4:30 the following afternoon. Bone and Loraine were in the Sheriff's office having coffee and visiting with Mason, Fiona and Lucy.

Mason, Fiona, Lucy, Mary Lou and Cletus had made the short trip out to the Broken Diamond F ranch with Mason under a tarp in the back and returned in the middle of the morning.

Mary Lou had forced her husband, Cletus to take her shopping.

"I want ya'll to know just how rough riding layin' down in the back of a buckboard. Thank God I only have one more trip to make."

"We'll have to bring Lawson Crane, the undertaker, over here and clue him in so he can prepare a casket for tomorrow," said Fiona.

"Can't wait," commented Mason sarcastically.

"We can handle that," said Bone, rubbing his temples. "Think I overdid it with the Cactus Wine last night. My head feels like it has two bobcats in a sack inside." Bone took a sip of the very stout coffee Loraine had brewed.

Lucy got up from her place in the floor beside Newton and approached Bone. "You should have said something...here." She put her hands on either side of Bone's head over his close-cropped dark hair. "Close your eyes."

He closed his eyes and relaxed as a bright blue glow emanated seemingly from underneath Lucy's hands. She held them there for a moment, and then took them away.

"How's that?" she asked.

"Dang, I forgot all about that." Bone blinked a couple of times. "Gone...Completely gone."

"How many times did you do that to me, Bone?"

He looked at Loraine. "Twice. Once in the stage trying to get the bleeding stopped and the air escaping from your lung where that .45 had clipped it. Then again after the doc sewed you up and went to bed to try to get your temperature down...I was better with it the second time."

Loraine walked across the room, held each side of Bone's face, and kissed him full on the mouth for what seemed to the others like an inordinately long time. "I didn't say thank you yesterday."

Bone's face froze with the just kissed look for a long moment. His stared straight ahead, his eyes not blinking.

"You all right, Bone?" Flynn finally asked. "Don't think I've ever seen you speechless."

The question broke his reverie. "Huh? What?…Oh,…uh, yeah, I'm fine." He looked over at Loraine for another moment and muttered softly, "Daaaumn."

"Breathe, Bone," said Fiona.

"Oh!…Right."

He took a breath and blinked his eyes twice again, but never taking them off Loraine's.

"What's Cactus Wine?" asked Fiona, smiling, breaking the moment.

Loraine grinned at Bone, and then turned to Fiona. "Well, it's not really wine…It's one hundred percent blue agave tequila and peyote tea from Mexico."

"Oh, my God," exclaimed Mason. "That has to be lethal…or near to it."

"Ya think," said Bone, then he looked at Loraine again. "How come you didn't get hung over, Pard?"

She grinned at him again and winked. "I'll never tell."

§§§

CHAPTER TWENTY-FIVE

SHERIFF'S OFFICE

"That sounds like the stage," said Flynn as he glanced up at the Regulator wall clock. "Made good time, it's only 4:30...Ya'll best get out and welcome our friends.

"Yep, I'd say so," said Bone.

He got to his feet, slid the steel bolt in the door back and opened it for Loraine and the others, making sure he was hiding behind it.

"Put on a good show," said Flynn as he locked the door after they left.

Fiona got her hanky out to dab her eyes while they all walked down toward the stage as it came to a halt in front of the depot and telegraph office next door to the Coolwater Saloon.

Bodie, Jack and Selden trotted up alongside the coach.

Jack leaned over to the window. "We're goin' to take the boys on down to Mom's Livery an' we'll be right back up."

"It's the bags we'll be gettin' while you're doin' that, husband," said Angie, in her Irish brogue, as she turned the handle and pushed the door open.

"There's Bone an' them comin' down the street from the sheriff's office," commented Bodie.

"Is Fiona with them?" asked Annabel from inside the coach.

"She is...an' doesn't look real good," said Bodie as he and the marshals trotted their horses down the street toward Mom's.

"Oh, bless her heart, I wouldn't think so," Annabel replied.

She and Angie stepped down on the single metal step, and then to the street, followed by Doctor Winchester.

The jehu, Charlie Mitchell, was on top of the coach handing the baggage down to Pearly Clark, the shotgun messenger on the near side.

The driver turned and started to climb down when he saw Bone and Loraine coming down the boardwalk with Fiona and Lucy.

"Well, pee on the fire an' call the dogs...I don't believe it," Charlie said as the group reached the stage.

"Shore didn't expect to see you up an' about, little lady," Pearly commented to Loraine. "You bein' shot an' all."

"She's tougher than shoe leather," said Bone.

"If that ain't a fact, God's a possum," added Charlie.

Loraine glanced at Bone. "Shoe leather?"

He shrugged his wide shoulders.

"What do you mean, shot?" asked Doctor Winchester.

"We had to take care of some highway men the other day north of town. Loraine got clipped...Doc Mosier fixed her up," said Bone.

"Curtis Mosier?" asked Winchester.

"Yep, office is right down there." Bone pointed.

"I'll have to go down and talk to him. We were in medical school together."

"Small world," said Bone.

Annabel hugged Fiona. "Oh, Fiona, honey, bless your heart, I am so sorry. I've been prayin' for you."

Fiona sniffed and wiped her eyes with her hanky. "Thank you so much, Annabel." She turned and hugged Angie, and then blew her nose.

Jack, Bodie and Selden walked up, with their hats in their hands and offered their condolences to Fiona.

"Charlie, you and Pearly mind taking their bags across the street to the hotel?" asked Bone.

"We kin do that I 'magine...Then gotta take the team down to Mom's. We're not leavin' out till of the mornin' fer Breckenridge."

"Well, ya'll have a drink on me over at the Coolwater. Tell Truman to put it on my account," added Bone.

"We kin shore do that, cain't we, Pearly?"

"Do believe...an' thankee kindly, Deputy Bone," said Pearly.

"Folks, lets go down to the sheriff's office. There's something ya'll need to see," commented Bone.

"Are you sure you're all right, Loraine?" asked *Anompoli Lawa* as they walked.

"Oh, yes, Bone worked some of Lucy's magic on me. I feel fine, just still a little weak from the blood loss, but not bad, though. My motor feels the same, but my tank is not as big as normal."

"Not sure I understand that last part, but it sounds good," replied Doctor Winchester.

"I think Lucy linked up with me to help, didn't you, Lucy?" asked Bone.

She smiled, demurely. "A little."

"Ah, of course. Well, be sure to drink plenty of fluids for the next few days," he cautioned. "If it's all right, I think I'll stop in and see Doctor Mosier."

"Uh, why don't you come on down to the office for a couple of minutes first...It's important," suggested Bone.

Winchester looked at the big man with a puzzled expression. "If you say so."

They reached the front door of the sheriff's office and Bone knocked three times. "We're back," he said through the door.

The bolt shot back and the door opened inward. Jack and Selden exchanged glances.

"Well, that's odd," commented Bodie as they couldn't see anyone.

The door closed behind them when everyone was inside. They turned to see Mason, with a smile on his face.

"Mason! What the Sam Hill?" exclaimed Jack.

"Bone, you want to fill everybody in before they go into a state of apoplexy?" said Mason.

"Yep. Ya'll find a place to light, this may take a few minutes."

"...and that's pretty much where we stand at this point," said Bone some thirty minutes later. "You're saying that there's no way the Johnson boy could be involved, that right, Selden?"

He exchanged glances with Jack. "That's the way we see it, Bone. One, his beat up old Sharps was about to fall apart, two, his spavined horse would never make to Texas, much less back."

"Three, he's a good kid who's a bit embarrassed an' ashamed about his papa...Not so his mama. She blames the law for her situation," added Jack.

"So that leaves Cobb an' the widow Waverly...an' you say she's wheelchair bound an' apparently rich as old ben gump," said Mason.

"Is it possible she could have hired someone?" asked Fiona.

"That is a definite possibility," said Loraine.

"Well, that's the purpose of this whole charade...to see if we can smoke out the perp. My gut says they're going to show at the funeral...We just have to be ready," added Bone. "It's been Loraine and my experience that serial killers have a degree of ego that's most always involved."

"I agree," commented Fiona.

"So do Selden an' me," said Jack.

"Guess I have to go along with that, too," added Mason.

"Lucy, do you think you could tell if the killer is present?" asked Bone. "I mean like you know what's going on with me?"

"Probably not, Bone....Senders like you, Fiona and Mason are really quite rare at this stage of your species development." Lucy thought for a moment.

"All I got just before they fired at Mason was a feeling of evil close by...It was like a cold darkness."

Bone paced back and forth across the room a couple of times, and then said, "All right, here's what we're going to do..."

Cletus glanced at his silver pocket watch to note the time was nine o'clock. The morning broke cloudy with a cold drizzle as he pulled up behind Lawson Crane, the undertaker's building, in his buckboard.

His wife, Mary Lou, Fiona and Lucy had gotten off at the sheriff's office while he continued to Crane's with Mason under the tarp in the back.

He glanced up and down the narrow alleyway in back before he set the brake and clambered down.

Lawson Crane had heard him drive up and opened the man door beside the wide opening with split double doors to the inside where he kept his hearse.

His team of black Tennessee Walkers were already hitched up and his best coffin was in the back of his enameled black, glass-sided hearse. The horses were hitched to the ornate carriage with all black harness and black and white feather plumes on their headstalls.

Cletus pulled back the tan tarp in the back that was covering Mason Flynn, dressed in his best suit. His dark hair was slicked down with Dapper Dan pomade and Fiona had applied a light tan makeup before they left the ranch.

He stepped down to the ground from the open tailgate, nodded to Crane who opened the back of the hearse, and then the front half of the walnut stained and varnished coffin.

Mason took a breath and clambered inside the white satin lined death box, looked at the undertaker and said, "All right, Lawson, let's do this. How long to get to the Baptist Church?"

"'Bout ten minutes, Sheriff. Got six pall bearers to take you inside, Deputy Bone, Marshals McGann and Lindsey, Texas Ranger Bodie Hickman, your brother in law, Cletus, here and your other deputy, Gomer Platt…Just relax."

"Easy for you to say, you're not in a coffin."

"Well, that's right, I reckon…Leastwise not yet."

The skinny as a rail, cadaverous looking undertaker set his black top hat on his head and mounted the seat to his funerary vehicle.

He flicked the reins on the high-stepping horses. "Come up there, boys." They both snorted in anticipation of pulling the carriage to the church in a stately manner and pranced out of the building.

The team and hearse rounded the last corner, pulled up in front of the white shiplap steepled church where the pall bearers, all dressed in dark suits, white shirts with celluloid collars and cravats, waited.

Crane opened the back and the six men pulled the casket out, three to the side and walked slowly up the walkway to the open double front doors of the only Baptist church in Jacksboro.

Every pew was full of townsfolk, friends and acquaintances. Mason's wife, family and close friends were in the front pews on both sides.

They carried the casket down the wide aisleway to the front and set it on the black satin draped table at the front. Crane opened the front half of the lid to expose the body for viewing.

Deputy Marshal McGann's wife Angie, stood on the dais with a single lily in her hands against her bosom. Accompanied by the robed church choir and organist, she began to sing Sheriff Flynn's favorite hymn: the pre-civil war Negro spiritual,

Just a Closer Walk With Thee

I am weak but Thou art strong
Jesus keep me from all wrong
I'll be satisfied as long
As I walk, let me walk close to Thee…
Just a closer walk with Thee
Grant it, Jesus, is my plea
Daily walking close to Thee
Let it be, dear Lord, let it be…
When my feeble life is o'er
Time for me will be no more
Guide me gently, safely o'er
To Thy kingdom's shore, to Thy shore…
Just a closer walk with Thee
Grant it, Jesus, is my plea
Daily walking close to Thee
Let it be, dear Lord, let it be.

Tears ran down Angie's face along with much of the audience as her clear, lyrical soprano voice filled the auditorium with the beautiful lyrics.

§§§

CHAPTER TWENTY-SIX

BAPTIST CHURCH
JACKSBORO, TEXAS

Pastor D. W. Jolley took the dais and stood behind the pulpit to introduce Bone.

"Deputy Darrell Ulysses Bone will deliver the eulogy." He looked down at the first row of friends and family and nodded. "Deputy Bone."

The big man, dressed in a new dark blue suit, white shirt with a stiff celluloid collar that made him look almost like he was wearing his Marine Corps dress blues, climbed the two steps to the dais and took his place behind the pulpit.

"Friends, family and neighbors, we are here today to honor and celebrate the life of Sheriff Mason Lee Flynn. I said celebrate his life…not to mourn his death…is what he would have wanted."

He looked down at Fiona in the first pew. "His bride of only a few months, Fiona Mae Miller Flynn is pregnant with their first child and I know one of his great regrets would be that he didn't live to see his child."

He looked out over the audience, many of whom were still wiping the tears from their eyes from the song and noted several women dressed in black with dark veils. Lucy looked back at him and nodded.

Bone was surprised to see Cherokee Cobb sitting in the last pew at the back of the auditorium, but he didn't show that emotion. The man was dressed in a worn sack cloth dark suit and a once white shirt with no tie. On the opposite side of the room, at the end of a pew, sat a woman in a tall wicker-backed wheelchair.

"Mason Flynn devoted his life to serving his country and his fellow man. From his fourteen years as a United States Cavalry officer to his seven years as the sheriff of Jack County, Texas.

He lost his first wife, Elizabeth Ann, who was also pregnant with their first child when she was kidnapped and murdered by a group of Comancheros.

"After tracking down and killing all eight members of the gang...That loss prompted him to run for sheriff after working with a group of men in north Texas known as the Trackers. A professional posse, hired to track down and arrest, when possible, the worst, most bloodthirsty outlaws in the area...the murderers, rapists and robbers.

"Mason devoted himself to public service with no thought of his own life. As sheriff, he tracked down a robber and murderer...and he was forced to defend himself when the man resisted arrest...He had to kill his own twin brother."

A low murmur swept the church.

"I came to respect Mason Flynn as a great law officer, mentor and almost as a father figure." Bone paused. "He was a good man." His voice broke a little.

"Rivers shouldn't flood...tornadoes shouldn't tear things up...the good shouldn't die young..."

"You lie! screeched the woman in black, wearing a black veil, seated in the wheelchair—the widow Corine Waverly. "He was a despicable murderer of young boys."

She rolled her chair up to the front, crossed over to the center of the aisleway, spun and faced Bone and the casket on the dais. "I hope you burn in hell! And I hope your wife and child suffer like I have and die...You worthless bastard!"

The stunned audience broke their reverie, whispering to each other.

Fiona got to her feet, walked over, stood in front of the woman and ripped the veil away. The widow's wrinkled face snarled at her.

"I'll kill you!"

"Maybe you'd like to try me again," said Mason as he sat up in his coffin, staring straight at Corine Waverly.

The auditorium erupted in screams, several women fainted. Those close to the aisleway jumped to their feet, rushed to the back and burst through the doors to the outside.

"Damn you!" The widow turned, got easily to her feet with a .40 caliber Colt Thunderer she had pulled from under the blanket covering her legs. She held it in her hand and aimed at Fiona as Mason was stepping out of the casket. "Since he can't die…You will."

A loud roar filled the church. The widow flipped backward turning her chair over. She landed on top of it, crumpled up like wet newspaper and lay still.

Bone stood next to Mason, his .50 caliber Smith & Wesson 500 still in his hand with just a thin tendril of smoke curling from the barrel.

He turned toward the gold cross mounted on the wall behind the choir. "Forgive me, Lord, for violating your sanctity." A tear rolled down his cheek.

Loraine, already on her feet, ran up on the dais and hugged the big man.

"I never had to shoot a woman before, Pard," he said with his voice cracking. "And in a house of God, too."

Bone turned to a still stunned preacher. "I'm sorry Reverend Jolley, I broke the sixth commandment...in God's temple, no less. I am so sorry, please forgive me." He dropped to his knees in front of him and his body shook with sobs.

Reverend Jolley put his hand on his shoulder. "You didn't break God's commandment, son. The sixth commandment says 'Thou shalt not commit murder...Murder is defined as: the unlawful premeditated killing of one human being by another...You had no choice. You saved two lives, maybe more, by killing an evil person. She reeked of it...I forgive you for doing it in my church and I'm sure God forgives you, too...I'm glad you told me the purpose of this ahead of time...What did you call it?"

"Charade," said Bone.

The preacher nodded. "Charade...Now rise up, son...Let's see if we can get this cleaned up." He smiled. "At least the undertaker is already here."

"Did you know she might be armed," asked Fiona.

Bone shook his head. "In any moment of decision or crises, the best thing you can do is usually the right thing...and the next best thing is usually the wrong thing...and the worst thing you can do...is nothing." He smiled. "Bone's law."

"Glad you were armed, Bone," said Mason as they all gathered in a private dining room in Sewell's Restaurant. "I didn't think about the killer goin' off the rails in the church house."

"We have a card that's used for instant credit in our time. They have an advertising slogan…Never go anywhere without it…There's been a few fellows in our time who went in and shot up a church during services. If just one of the parishioners had been packing…they could have stopped it."

"How did you know it was the widow?" asked Fiona.

"Didn't…Like I mentioned earlier, I had a gut feeling, plus, following Sherlock Holmes dictum, 'Once you eliminate the impossible, whatever remains, no matter how improbable, must be the truth.' So, when Pard and I investigated where the sniper was up in the rocks near the Broken Diamond F Ranch, we found where they went to the bathroom."

"So," questioned Loraine.

"Elementary, my dear Loraine, elementary...See, when a man pees, he'll kind of wave it around a bit. Even to the point of writing his name in snow..."

"Bone!" exclaimed Fiona.

"Well, it's true...done it myself. So, anyway, where they went, if you'll remember..." He looked at Loraine. "There was a hole in the wet spot about the size of a quarter in the middle of the damp sand. I mentioned that I wondered why they didn't pee on the side of the rock."

"Good point," said Jack.

"Show everyone the pictures we took up there, Pard.

"Loraine pulled out her smart phone and went to the photo gallery, scrolled across to the pictures of that scene and held it up, showing the wet sand and hole.

"That's amazing," said Mason.

"Then I also noted some snuff spittle on the rock. Now, Bass had told us before that snuff spit is thinner and lighter than chewing tobacco...See how thin it is in the picture."

Loraine passed the phone in front of everyone.

"Your point," said Fiona.

"When I went out to the widow's, I noticed one of the lines at the corner of her mouth was a bit darker than the others…My grandmother, on my daddy's side, dipped snuff and she would never let anyone see her, but there was always one of the wrinkles at the corner of her mouth that was dark."

"I'd have never noticed that," said Jack.

"I would, me husband…How often have I caught you with your chaw," Angie pointed to the smile lines at the corners of his mouth under his dark mustache."

He nodded. "Guilty as charged, love." He kissed her on the cheek.

"Then when she took the shot a Mason, I saw a rider galloping off to the east on a bay horse…There were two in the paddock beside the barn at her ranch when I rode in. One had saddle lines and dried sweat on his back. She said all the hands were out with the cattle…She hadn't taken the time to brush her horse down after the hard ride from town."

"It could have been one of the hands who had come in an' was still in the barn," offered Selden.

"Could have, but I noticed that her lace-up ankle boots had horse manure on the side of the sole."

"So if she were wheelchair bound, why would there be horse manure on her shoes?" affirmed Loraine.

"Bingo, Pard...Now show everyone the two pictures of her fingerprints."

Loraine scrolled over to two pictures side by side of fingerprints. "One of them is the one I pulled from that casing Bone found on top of the bank building and the other I took from her hand afterwards at the church with my small makeup mirror I had in my purse...I checked it when we went back to the hotel to change clothes." She passed the phone around again.

"No two people have the same fingerprints...that was the pièce de résistance that proves she was the shooter," said Bone.

"Gotta learn how to do that," said Mason.

"Absolutely," agreed Fiona.

"Count me in," added Jack.

"Me four," said Selden.

"And five," commented Bodie.

Sure will save a lot of evildoers from walking out of court," said Fiona.

"We'll get the materials, make each of you a crime scene kit and teach you how to use it," commented Bone.

"Except you won't get one of these." Loraine held up her smart phone. "They won't be available for another one hundred ten years or so."

"Say, when you going to show me some of that Kung Fu, stuff, Pard?"

"What time is it?"

"Oh, about class time, I would say," he said.

"Why don't ya'll do it down at the city park next to the creek?" suggested Mason. "Plenty of shade and grass to fall on."

Loraine grinned. "May be some of that...Lead the way, Sheriff."

§§§§

EPILOGUE

SEWELL PARK

Bone and Loraine had donned their Apache style moccasins and were in an expansive grassy area beside Spiller's Branch. They were surrounded by Mason, Fiona, Lucy, Mary Lou, Cletus, Selden,

Jack and Angie, Bodie and Annabel, Doctor Ashalatubbi, Gomer and Emma Lou.

"I brought my medical kit, if you need it, Bone," said Winchester.

"Not likely," he said as he moved to the center of the circle in front of Loraine.

"Okay, Pard, lets do it."

"Since Kung Fu is primarily defensive, I want you to try to grab me."

"Huh?…If you wish."

He rushed at her like a linebacker going in for a tackle. She sidestepped, stuck her leg in front of his, tripping him to fall on his face in the grass. Loraine spun in a 360 degree circle and stopped facing him again.

"Good one, Pard."

He got to his feet, jumped in the air parallel to the ground, throwing his hip straight at her head, like a flying body block. Loraine ducked under his 285 pounds, letting him fall rolling across the ground.

"That's two," she said.

"And that's all," countered Bone.

"Try to hit me," Loraine said.

"Aw, come on, Pard, I don't want to hurt you."

"You won't."

He took a round house swing at her, she ducked again, grabbed his wrist and pulled him forward to where he lost his balance and fell to his face again.

"All right, I'm through playing, Pard," said Bone.

He didn't rush her, but crouched like a wrestler, shuffling forward—his hands shot out like a pair of cottonmouths and he grabbed her shoulders. She brought her arms up inside his, knocking his hands away, then she grabbed the sides of his head over his ears, threw herself backward to the ground with her foot in his stomach and pushed, still holding on to his head.

He flew in the air almost eight feet, landing on his back with a whoosh as all of his air was knocked out of him.

"Ahh, ahh." He rolled from side to side trying to get some air.

Loraine straddled him, put both hands under his combat belt and lifted him a couple of times, pulling air into his starving lungs.

"Bone, honey, are you all right? Say something."

"I give," he wheezed. "I give...King's X."

She covered his mouth with kisses, which he returned with fervor. Loraine finally came up for air.

"I love you, Bone."

"I love you, too, Pard."

"You call me 'Loraine' at the stage."

"You heard me?"

She nodded. "You also called me 'baby' and 'honey' and prayed to God for me to live. I thought I was dreaming, but now I know you said those things."

"Well, I…"

"You held me in your arms for over five hours and said, 'Don't leave me, baby'."

He grinned and looked up into her limpid brown eyes. "I love you, Loraine…Always have."

"Damn you, Bone." She whacked him across the chest with her fist. "Why haven't you said anything before now?"

They were both oblivious to the twelve people encircling them, listening with rapt attention. Lucy's face was beaming like a beacon.

"It's a long story, Pard."

"Out with it, Bone, or I'm going to have to hurt you."

"Calf rope, Loraine."

She sat back, still straddling his broad chest.

"Come on, you're stalling."

"When I was in college, I was one of the stars of the football team and I fell for the head twirler...I mean head over heels. We dated almost all through the football season and after the last game, I walked out in the parking lot to find her...You sure you want to hear this?"

"Talk, mister."

"I found her in a car talking with her old boyfriend from high school. Well, she got out, looked up at me and said, 'You never forget your first love, Bone...Randy was my boyfriend back home."

"So?"

"There's no mystery with you. I know exactly what you're thinking...You don't make me wonder...You're just not exciting...You're an open book...I can't date you anymore.' Then she said the killer. 'You're a nice guy, but girls don't always want nice guys...They want to wonder......Good bye, Bone.' She turned and got back in his car." He took a deep breath. "I haven't let a girl inside since."

"She was a fool…So that was the reason for the Donald Trump wall?"

"Pretty much."

"Well, I got news for you, big boy…I don't want to wonder, I want to know what you're thinking every minute of the day like I want you to know what I'm thinking…I like open books…I love you, you big lug…I love your honesty…I love that you can't hide anything from me…Does that answer your final question?"

"You know there was a song released the first time in 1959, entitled *My Heart is an Open Book* by Carl Dobkins, Jr. and one of the lines was, 'Look, look, My heart is an open book, I love nobody but you'. I thought that was the way it was supposed to be."

"It is, dufus…No, she was the dufus…Do you know every song that was ever written?"

Bone grinned, put his hands under her arms and stood up, lifting her along with him and set her on the ground at his feet. He picked her up again, held her to his chest with her feet over a foot from the ground, and kissed her, long and hard.

She returned his kiss, matching and even exceeding his passion. They finally broke apart to applause from their friends—and with extra emotion from Lucy who was jumping up and down.

They looked around, and then back at each other, finally realizing they weren't alone and grinned.

"What the hell," they said simultaneously and kissed again.

§§§§

PREVIEW OF THE
NEXT EXCITING BONE NOVEL

BONE & LORAINE

CHAPTER ONE

SKEANS BOARDING HOUSE
GAINESVILLE, TEXAS

"What are you so nervous about, Bone?" asked Jack McGann

Bone tugged at his starched collar. "Never did this before, Marshal."

"Neither had I 'fore Angie an' I got hitched."

"Where did they perform the ceremony?"

"At Angie's house up in the Arbuckles," said Jack. "But, I was more nervous about who was doin' it."

"Who was that?" asked Bone.

"The Judge…Judge Isaac Parker."

"Ooo, see what you mean. Would have liked to met him. Heard he was a great man."

Jack nodded. "Passed away in '96, brights disease. He could look right through you. Knowed when you were lyin', too…One time, he was tryin' a colored feller fer murder an' they found him guilty. The Judge sentenced him to hang an' the feller's attorney jumped up an' run up to protest to the Judge that the sentence was too harsh." Jack chuckled. "Well, the Judge jest pointed his finger at the man an' he fell to the floor almost in a state of apoplexy an' laid there till the Judge entered his chambers…Judge Parker never said a word to 'im…jest pointed his finger at him."

"Dang, that would have been a sight to see," said Bone as he looked over at the archway covered with branches from a female juniper, loaded with cones of ripe purple berries, and a large sprig of mistletoe hung from the center.

BONE & LORAINE

It was placed in front of a number of wooden folding chairs with a center aisle between them.

The wedding of Bone and Loraine was being held in Faye Skeans' back yard, the same place where Sheriff Mason Flynn and Deputy US Marshal Fiona Mae Miller, Bone's great grand parents, were married last spring and Walt Durbin and Frances Ann Sullivant were married two years before that.

Doctor Winchester Ashalatubbi, also known by his Chickasaw tribal name of *Anompoli Lawa*—it means, He Who Talks to Many—was performing the ceremony in his capacity as a Doctor of Divinity, like he did for Mason and Fiona. His credentials as a Doctor of Divinity were in addition to his degree as a physician and his position as the Shaman, or spiritual leader, of the Chickasaw tribe.

Jack has been know to say, 'Winchester can birth you, marry you, doctor you and your spirit, and bury you'.

Anompoli Lawa was taking his place in the center of the arch as Angie sang the wedding march to the accompaniment of Marshal Loss Hart on the fiddle. He was dressed in a traditional beaded white doeskin war shirt of the Chickasaw Nation and holding his worn black leather covered Bible.

Loraine stepped out of the back door of Faye's three story, red brick, Queen Ann style house in a beautiful white satin gown, tight around her wasp waist with white ruffled lace around the top of her bodice and over her shoulders. Jack and Angie's adopted daughter, ten year old Aurali Red, carried the dress' long train.

Bone had taken his place in front of and to the left of Doctor Ashalatubbi. His knees almost buckled when he saw Loraine step out of the door.

Her lustrous long black hair shined in the late afternoon sun on this bright and clear fall day, only slightly enhanced with a small amount of brilliantine. It was done up in Newport coiffure with a spiral bun on top of a French twist held by pins and two pearl combs. The rest of Loraine's hair was in tight ring curls on both sides and short ones for her bangs. She was stunning.

Mason, acting as Bone's Best Man, leaned over to the big man. "Close your mouth, Bone, you'll catch flies."

"Oh, right."

"But, I don't blame you. Loraine could stop a war."

"Or start one," added Bone.

BONE & LORAINE

Loraine was being given away by the legendary Deputy US Marshal Bass Reeves, while Fiona Mae Flynn was her Matron of Honor.

The chairs were filled with a number of people from Gainesville, Jacksboro and the Nations. They included, Deputy US Marshal Selden Lindsey, Angie and Deputy US Marshal Jack McGann, with Baby Sarah. Walt and Frances Durbin with their toddler, Lisanne Gifford, Buster Martin and Slim Parker were on one side of the aisle.

Texas Ranger Bodie Hickman, his wife Annabel and their twins, Bass and Cassie Ann, Deputy Gomer Platt and his intended Emma Lou Burke were on the other, along with some of Faye's friends and neighbors. They all were turned in their chairs watching Loraine, Bass and Aurali Red step stately down the aisle to the music. Loraine carried a bouquet of purple aster flowers with a yellow center—similar to a daisy.

Loraine stopped in front of *Anompoli Lawa*, handed her flowers to Fiona and turned to face Bone.

Doctor Ashalatubbi began, "We are gathered here today in the sight of God, and the presence of friends and loved ones, to celebrate one of life's greatest moments. We are here to give recognition to the beauty of love that is shared between Bone and Loraine and as they complete their family in holy matrimony. Marriage is a contract not to be entered into lightly…"

He finished the invocation, the prayer and the exchange of vows, and then asked for the rings.

"May we now have the rings?"

Bodie and Annabel's twins, Bass and Cassie had walked up behind Loraine and Bone with tiny satin pillows. There was a plain gold band in the center of each.

"The ring, an unbroken circle, represents unending love. As often as either of you look upon these rings, may you be reminded of this moment and the love you have promised to one another. Darrel Ulysses Bone, please place this ring on Loraine's finger and repeat your commitments."

"Loraine, I give you this ring as a symbol of my love and that I'm choosing to share my life's journey with you. I give you this ring with the pledge to love you today, tomorrow, and always."

"Now, Loraine Maria Rodriguez, please place this ring on Bone's finger and repeat your commitments."

BONE & LORAINE

"Bone, I give you this ring as a symbol of my love and that I'm choosing to share my life's journey with you I give you this ring with the pledge to love you today, tomorrow, and always."

"Bone and Loraine, I want to wish you both much love and happiness as you begin your new journey. Remember to keep lots of laughter in your life and love will never be far behind…"

"No problem there," muttered Loraine.

Winchester smiled, then continued, "Now Bone and Loraine, you have pledged your faith to each other in the company of your family and friends.

"By the power vested in me by the State of Texas, I now pronounce you husband and wife.

"Bone, you may now kiss your beautiful bride…Family and friends, I am proud to present for the first time as husband and wife…Mr. and Mrs. Bone."

Bone picked Loraine up off the ground, held her to him and kissed her, her feet dangling in the air. She returned the kiss.

After a moment, *Anompoli Lawa* cleared his throat. Bone and Loraine broke their kiss, glanced at the venerable Shaman and both blushed. He set her down to the applause of the attendees.

"What's the matter, can't ya'll wait," commented Mason with a chuckle as he slapped Bone on the back.

The ladies all gathered around Loraine to give her a hug and well wishes while the men congratulated Bone. A stainless steel flask was soon produced and began making the rounds.

Bone took the flask and looked at Jack. "This isn't Cactus Wine, is it?"

Jack looked puzzled. "Since I have no idee what that is, no…This is good old Kentuck sour mash."

"Whew, good thing…Tell you about Cactus Wine sometime," Bone replied and turned the flask up.

"You got me interested, Bone, what is it?" asked Jack.

Bone grinned. "Tequila and peyote tea."

"My God in Heaven."

You got that right," replied Bone.

Loraine walked over to Bone from talking with the ladies, jumped up, threw her arms around his neck and gave him a big kiss, and then leaned back. "I can't believe I'm now going to be called, 'Mrs. Bone'. Oh, my God…Who knew? Bone and Mrs.

324

Bone…Guess it's going to be like, Mr. and Mrs. North."

"Except we're not amateur detectives, Mrs. Bone…We're professionals."

"True, Mr. Bone," Loraine replied.

"Ya'll goin' any place for your honeymoon?" asked Mason.

"Bodie suggested Hot Springs, Arkansas," said Bone looking at Loraine.

"I understand it's an interestin' place to relax…an'…"

"What are you talking about, mister?" asked Mason's wife, Deputy US Marshal Fiona Flynn.

"Just said I heard the Hot Springs was a good place to go for a honeymoon…dear."

"Uh-huh. Why haven't we ever gone there? Fact is, why haven't we ever gone anywhere for a honeymoon?"

"Uh…"

"Say, why don't ya'll go there with us? We'll make it a double honeymoon." He looked down at Loraine again.

She smiled and nodded.

"Dang, Bone, why didn't I think of that?" said Mason.

Fiona's steel-gray eyes drilled her husband. "I was thinking the exact same thing, Mister Flynn."

"Well, Missus Flynn, would you like to take our long delayed honeymoon to Hot Springs, Arkansas?"

She smiled. "Though you'd never ask."

§§

Wonder what's going to happen on this trip? - Ken Farmer

TIMBER CREEK PRESS

BLACKSTAR BAY by T.C. Miller
BLACKSTAR MOUNTAIN by T.C. Miller

HISTORICAL FICTION WESTERN
THE NATIONS by Ken Farmer and Buck Stienke
HAUNTED FALLS by Ken Farmer and Buck Stienke
HELL HOLE by Ken Farmer
ACROSS the RED by Ken Farmer and Buck Stienke
BASS and the LADY by Ken Farmer and Buck Stienke
DEVIL'S CANYON by Buck Stienke
LADY LAW by Ken Farmer
BLUE WATER WOMAN by Ken Farmer
FLYNN by Ken Farmer
AURALI RED by Ken Farmer
COLDIRON by Ken Farmer
STEELDUST by Ken Farmer
BONE by Ken Farmer
BONE'S LAW by Ken Farmer

SY/FY
LEGEND of AURORA by Ken Farmer & Buck Stienke
AURORA: INVASION (Book #6 in the BEF) by Ken Farmer & Buck Stienke

HISTORICAL FICTION ROMANCE
THE TEMPLAR TRILOGY
MYSTERIOUS TEMPLAR by Adriana Girolami
THE CRIMSON AMULET by Adriana Girolami
TEMPLAR'S REDEMPTION by Adriana Girolami

Coming Soon

HISTORICAL FICTION WESTERN
NO TIME to DIE by Buck Stienke
BONE & LORAINE by Ken Farmer

HISTORICAL FICTION ROMANCE
DAUGHTER of HADES by Adriana Girolami
ZAMINDAR and the LADY by Adriana Girolami

MILITARY ACTION/TECHNO
BLACKSTAR ENIGMA by T.C. Miller

SY/FY
ANTAREAN DILEMMA by T.C. Miller

Thanks for reading *BONE'S LAW*. If you enjoyed it, I would really appreciate a review on Amazon. My Author Page is:
www.amazon.com/Ken-Farmer/e/B0057OT3YI
Email - pagact@yahoo.com

Personally autographed books available at my web site:
Web page: www.KenFarmer-Author.net

TIMBER CREEK PRESS